THE TETRAD GROUP

RACING THE
WHIRLWIND

JANUARY BAIN

Racing the Whirlwind
ISBN # 978-1-83943-834-9
©Copyright January Bain 2020
Cover Art by Erin Dameron-Hill ©Copyright January 2020
Interior text design by Claire Siemaszkiewicz
Totally Bound Publishing

Totally Bound Publishing books by January Bain

Brass Ring Sorority
Winning Casey
Chasing Lacey
Romancing Rebecca

TETRAD Group
Racing Peril
Racing the Tide
Racing the Whirlwind

Manitoba Tea & Tarot Mysteries
Magic, Mayhem & Murder
Movies, Moonlight & Magic

RACING THE WHIRLWIND

Dedication

A book is always a journey that requires a great deal of support. I have been very pleased and honored to have the help of people I admire. From my incomparable editor, Rebecca Baker Fairfax, to the awesome team at Totally Bound Publishing, to the world's best husband for putting up with the time commitments such an undertaking requires, I give you all my most heartfelt thanks. You all do more good than you know.

Chapter One

"Whoever fights monsters should see to it that in the process he does not become a monster.
And if you gaze long enough into an abyss, the abyss will gaze back into you." — *Friedrich Nietzsche*

Alysia Rossini peered through the windshield of her Dodge RAM at the weather, which was growing fouler by the second. Her hands were clamped so tight to the steering wheel that her knuckles ached. The painted lines delineating the watery pavement had long vanished. Desperate to keep the vehicle on the road, she leaned in closer to the dash, her clothes damp and clammy from the perspiration that trickled down her spine. She had the wipers cranked to their highest setting, yet they were unable to keep up with the deluge of sleeting rain lashing the thick glass in heavy gusts. Her stomach churned with worry and the terrible sense of foreboding disquiet that had crept in during the hour-long journey, fueled by her intense isolation.

The hazy, gray, uncaring Cascade Mountains stretched out for hundreds of kilometers in all directions, looking like a distant planet. Driving home alone made Alysia hesitant to pull over. It was just as easy to get rear-ended on this treacherous highway as not. And that vehicle following behind was stalking too damn close. The driver needed their fucking head examined.

A few more tense kilometers inched by, Alysia clenching her hands tight to the wheel and flicking her glance at the rear-view mirror every few seconds. Her reduced speed kept her from hydroplaning the four-wheel-drive truck but increased the length of time with the idiot on her tail.

Finally, the squall began to ease, the lights of the vehicle behind her becoming more than just two white eyes glaring through the mist. Rolling her head from side to side, she worked to loosen the tenseness of her shoulders. The harsh reality of her twenty-four-hour work day followed by a visit with her friend Kate flashed through her mind, bringing with it added sadness and desperation—and an even more acute sense of isolation.

She shook her head, trying to shake the memories free. Reliving a nightmare loop never solved a damn thing. What she needed most was a drink. Ease from the pain of the job and Kate's devastating illness. Thank goodness it wasn't far to the gas station. She sped up, pressing her foot down on the pedal. The lights of the forecourt beckoned just ahead, sanctuary in a storm.

Oh, God no. The SUV following too damn close fishtailed in her rear-view mirror. It swayed side to side in a macabre dance, jerking back and forth like an artful pickpocket escaping the hands of justice. In slow motion, Alysia took in the horror of the vehicle beginning its death roll. It spun out of control, end over end, then came to rest on the side of the highway, belching billows of smoke.

She took her foot off the gas and swung the wheel to the right, preparing to turn around and pull to the side of the road near the stricken vehicle. No point in her having an accident as well.

She thrust her truck into park, glancing at the SUV ahead of her. Steam poured from the wreck in undulating waves. The wheels still spun, their fancy chrome hubcaps catching glimmers of light from her fog lamps.

Picking up her cell phone, she made the call.

"Nine-one-one, how may I help?" a voice on the other end of the lifeline asked in a calm, reassuring manner.

"Be advised there's a single vehicle accident on the Coquihalla, just north of the Great Bear snow sled, and five hundred meters south of the service station. I'm Alysia Rossini, trauma nurse with BC-STAR. The only one on scene. Vehicle rolled over about thirty seconds ago. Please call my crew and alert them to land in the parking lot at the gas station. Oh, and to watch for the overhead wires on the north side of the lot."

She glanced up again, a strange popping sound pulling her attention away from the operator recording her call. "Advise the vehicle's now on fire! I'm heading in!" She cut the call and thrust the phone into her jacket pocket. More help was on the way, but it wouldn't be for at least fifteen or twenty minutes. That was, if they could fly in this poor weather.

After grabbing a fire extinguisher and her portable trauma bag—a smaller version of her work kit— from the seat behind her, she opened the driver's door, stepping out onto the slippery roadway. Freezing rain pelted her head and shoulders, each stinging piece of water a harsh rebuke she took scant note of. The sight of flames emerging from near the front of the vehicle sent her adrenaline skyrocketing. She swallowed hard, focused on the next few precious moments of opportunity to save a human life from being snuffed out of existence.

She raced to the overturned SUV, her move second nature. Only tonight there was no secondary nurse running alongside her from the helicopter to the scene. She would be the only one providing the critical first few moments of assistance — often the difference between life and death.

She dropped her kit a few feet from the vehicle but held on to the fire extinguisher. Pulling off the metal firing pin, she directed the heavy red cannister's black hose at the undercarriage near the motor compartment, where bluish streaks of flame fueled by gasoline and rubber were shooting out and already rising higher.

How many people involved? She'd only seen the driver's head illuminated by dashboard lights, but that didn't mean there couldn't be others. *Please, please don't let there be children.* That was the worst. Innocent victims forever haunted their rescuers.

She took deep breaths to steady herself, taking in air permeated with the stench of burning oil and plastic. The dry chemical cloud meant to kill the flames only added to the stink, making her head ache.

She fought the flames, smothering them until nothing but dark smoke rolled off the wreck. The night became silent with the crackle of fire gone. No screams. Was the driver unconscious? *Or dead?*

She threw the empty container away and grabbed her emergency bag, dragging it closer on the freezing roadway. On her hands and knees, cold and wet seeping through her jeans, she approached the driver's door. Peering through the glass, she used her hand to swipe away the accumulated moisture. A man hung upside down from his seat, safety harness still in place, air bags deployed. No movement. She grabbed her flashlight from her kit and directed it inside. Just the one person. *Thank you, God.*

She reached for the door handle and tried jerking it open to find it stuck, hard.

"Damn it!" The expletive lowered her stress somewhat. A crowbar's image flashed into her brain. She raced back to her truck and located the one under the front seat. After racing back to the wreck, she slipped the tool into the crack between the door and the side panel and pried with all her might.

"Jaws of life would be handy right now," she muttered. She put her whole body into the action, all hundred and twenty-five pounds of sinew and muscle. She never neglected working out. Her job required a fit body. Unfortunately, she took most things to excess. A sudden memory of abusing alcohol at a convention the week before made her wince. Okay, so every responder on her crew had done the same, but she had to get a lid on things before her life spiraled right out of control.

The door gave way under her continued onslaught. Creaking in protest, it opened enough that she could squeeze her way inside. She placed her fingers on the man's neck, checking for a pulse. *Just detectable.* He was struggling, gasping for breath. Blood dripped from a large gaping cut on his forehead, accounting for his unconscious state. She needed to get oxygen into his system, fast.

"Are you okay?" she asked, trying to wake him. He looked to be in his late twenties or early thirties, close to her age, maybe a bit older, with curly dark hair that flopped over his eyes. He looked somewhat familiar, but she couldn't place him.

No response.

She didn't want to move him, not until help arrived and they could safely secure him to a backboard. That was one of the things she didn't carry. If there were unseen internal injuries or spinal fractures, she could do more damage. His body had been badly abused.

The harsh breathing stopped and her adrenaline spiked. *Cardiac arrest?*

She had to incubate him or he was at risk of brain damage. She moved away and opened her medical kit, pulling out a laryngoscope to locate his vocal cords, the entrance to his trachea. The bag also included the polyvinyl endotracheal tube with a balloon at the end required for the delicate operation. She needed to create a seal to prevent air from leaking out when she forced a breath with the portable suction bag, and to stop the patient from vomiting. It would be a tragedy to be saved, only to die of aspiration pneumonia days or weeks later.

Working upside down, all by herself, was going to make it challenging, if not impossible. But it wouldn't be the first time she'd had to jury-rig a device to work in the patient's favor. In the field, a nurse lived by her wits and quick ability to figure out what was necessary, or she washed out and left the profession for calmer waters.

Minutes slipped by. Alysia struggled to tube him, normally a two-person job. But then the hose cooperated and slipped down his trachea and into place. He was bagged. *Thank you, God.*

She began the process of getting life-giving air to his lungs. In and out. In and out. *Just breathe, that's it.*

How long until help arrives? BC-STAR air prided itself on lift-off being within five minutes of getting the call. No vehicles had gone by and no one had left the gas station to check. The fire couldn't have been large enough to be seen from that distance.

She looked into the man's face again, brushing back his wet hair to check the deep wound on his forehead that showed the white of bone. It dripped a steady stream of blood, almost black in the low light.

Who was he? The shape of his face haunted her. She was becoming more positive she knew the guy.

Then his eyes opened. Eyes that had haunted her since she was twelve years old stared back at her.

Oh. My. God. Time jerked to a punishing halt.

Not him.

Not the monster who had murdered her entire family. In cold blood. She wanted to yank the device out of his evil throat, to use it to strangle the life right out of him. Her hands froze in their self-appointed task. Her heart stuttered and her breathing grew harsh, forcing its way in strangled gasps from her horrified chest.

Was he stalking her? Was that why he'd been following so close behind her? No one would know if she just let him go into the good night, ended it right here and now. She could. She knew how. She had the means. Could anyone really blame her?

The police hadn't believed her all those years ago — said he'd had an airtight alibi in being away at that Ivy League school his parents had sent him to, to correct his behavior, to make better use of his intellect that tested right off the charts. But Alysia had always known he'd gotten away with murder, had taken revenge on her family for perceived harm to his own — a perception that had later proven unfounded.

And now he was back. At her mercy.

They stared at each other for a timeless moment. His eyes dark pools of emptiness, he gave no quarter. The decision was hers.

The roar of the helicopter engine overhead alerted her to incoming. She still had a couple of minutes yet — they had to get to the scene from the parking lot. There was still time to let the bastard die.

The staring contest continued for a few more deadly seconds. Her hand hesitated on the tube, wanting to yank it out. *Administer no aid. End it.* It wouldn't take much. Just hold her hand over his mouth and nose until all breathing ceased. His injuries would explain it.

The dilemma sliced into her brain. Pain followed. Her head felt about to explode with the acute stress. Her throat tightened. *No winning on this one.* Let him die — she lost. Let him live — she lost...

Chapter Two

One year later

Jeffrey Poe swiped the dripping sweat from his forehead with the back of a well-worn work glove, careful not to rub too hard at the sensitive scar tissue dividing his flesh from eyebrow to hairline. Though the temperature had remained below freezing with a brisk north wind coursing over the mountain pass, the effort required to fell a fourteen-inch-diameter tree with a chainsaw then de-limb it with an ax had overheated him. But the physical labor kept him strong, prepared, ready for anything this insane world could throw at him.

He stood and stretched his aching back, surveying his hard-won hewn-out parcel of timberland from a stranger's perspective. The view from this side of the mountain overlooking the meandering ribbon of river far below had settled in his bloodstream and made him feel invincible in his own isolated paradise. Sharp peaks iced with snow, rising to kiss the sky and as dangerous and majestic as ancient warriors guarding the past and present, surrounded his homestead.

It was inaccessible except for an overgrown logging road. He'd made certain there would be no unexpected visitors, installing motion-detectors and hidden closed-circuit cameras that would broadcast images of strangers into his recently-constructed yurt before he could see them with his naked eye, or through binoculars. He was proud of the yurt most of all. White sand-filled polyethylene coils stacked onto each succeeding ring until the proper height had been reached had created amazing insulating results. It looked like an Inuit's igloo while still letting in lots of light at the top and through the generous windows he'd installed. The place was as green as hell, with the impressive array of solar panels all placed at their proper angle nearby. Between the panels and burning wood, he didn't need hydro.

Living off-grid had turned out to be a whole lot of work, though now he was nearly there, never stronger or better prepared. He'd been at this venture for the better part of a year, but everything was almost finished now, in place. *Ready.* Never enough hours in the day for one pair of hands to do the myriad tasks, but he'd done it, if a few months later than planned. Of course, having to recuperate in hospital followed by weeks of convalescence, then dragging himself around the site trying to do all the work himself hadn't helped. But he'd done it, taken the pain.

He thought of all those jovial groups of friends and family that TV off-grid builders loved to depict as the norm on their show. *No fucking way. Didn't go that way.* He'd done this job all by himself. He was the one with the power. *The control.*

Looking over his land, getting a momentary twinge of satisfaction from the glorious view of the valley and winding river below, he shook his head. An immense surge of anger hit him, lightning-quick as always, making white light flash through his vision. It obscured everything else.

When his vision cleared enough to see, he directed the hot surge at the tree, hacking, and hacking some more, in efforts to remove all the bark and slimy disgusting moss. Bark would rot and be a host for insects. Chips of bark and green wood flew every which way, making him enraged when some stuck to his damp skin, making it itch. The odor of pine and skunk overloaded his olfactory senses, making his eyes water. The damn loathsome creature had invaded his territory today, leaving scent markings when his wolfdog had began barking in efforts to drive it away.

This was all her fucking fault. She was his unfinished baggage. She was the reason he'd fallen so far from grace. Why he was shunned by all those he'd counted on for a leg-up into the world of business and finance. One whiff of the stink she'd placed on him with her suspicions and all the rats had deserted him. And now look at him. Covered in dirt and sweat and exhausted from trying to make do all on his own. No one to help. *Well, fuck them.* If they ever asked for anything, he'd tell them where to shove it.

Payback was coming. His heart rate quickened when he thought of the underground crib he'd constructed to extend the game. No quick end this time. She owed him. One vow that wouldn't feel like work to make come true. A real-life game of chess, with the winner taking all.

Chapter Three

Day One

Creak.

What was that?

Alysia stopped in mid-twist, hand poised above the toilet tank handle, ready to flush. *There.* Another faint footpad. Someone was in the house, advancing down the hallway, step by cautious step. Not a nightmare, but real this time. Her mouth dry, her throat tightening, she tried to move. *Why, oh why didn't I kill him when I had the chance? Why did I resume CPR and save his evil ass? Because I swore to help others. It's why I went into nursing in the first place. And I didn't want to become like him.* The idealistic thought hadn't comforted her then and provided even less comfort now, because she had a terrible fear that if she had to do it all again, she might not come out the same person.

She couldn't unfreeze her body — every cell, every muscle, every fiber of her being was paralyzed by fear. The memory of another time slithered in between one heartbeat and the next, squeezing the life out of her like the pythons that she'd feared most when visiting the reptile house as a child. It pulled her under, took over. Filled her conscious mind with excruciating torment while her body remained frozen in place, bricked and mortared by the powerful image. *There.* A closer squeak of protest from the old wooden floorboards. A whiff of odor she couldn't identify. *Move, damn it!*

She broke free of the terror in a rush of self-preservation driven by a single gossamer strand of willpower. She picked up her cell phone sitting on the edge of the sink and lunged for the window, thrust up the lower pane with hands trembling to the point of not seeming under her control, and pushed one foot over the ledge to climb through the small space. Her heel caught on a sharp nail head protruding through the wood frame. She swallowed the hurt. Pulling her other foot up and over the sill, she jumped.

Dizzy from waves of night terrors flooding in with a vengeance, she padded across the icy asphalt shingles on bare feet. She forced herself to think, to remain in the moment. It would be too easy to succumb to her worst fear, to allow the past to sweep away all she had worked so hard to build. To just lie down and die, have it over with. The pain. The guilt. The sleepless nights.

Then the image of her father filled her brain, encouraging her to keep moving. *Don't let evil win, sweetheart.* Suddenly he was right there with her, beckoning her forward in the night, an in corporeal image hovering between life and death. Between this world and the next, comforting and bittersweet, because in her heart she knew it wasn't real. Instead he was lying in his grave by her mother's side hundreds of miles away.

Fortified by the vision, she halted at the edge of the roof and looked downward. It was at least twenty feet to the blurry ground below. *Why didn't I put on my glasses? Or bring the Beretta from the nightstand?* For the same reason she hadn't switched on the bathroom light—it was the middle of the night and there was no need. And bright lights bothered her over-sensitive eyes. She'd only brought her phone in case of an emergency at work or with Kate. *No hope for it now.* She had to go over the edge. Maybe the two feet of heavy snow would break her fall? *Or not.* Better a broken limb than what waited inside.

There would be no quick end to her life—she knew that with dead certainty. The realization made her push down the panic threatening to grab her by the throat and paralyze her yet again. Why hadn't she ended it all on the highway all those months ago? She shook her head. Too late for regrets. She knew it was him, back to finish the job. *The last witness.*

She eased her body down past the eaves and dangled in mid-air, her phone held precariously between her teeth. When her arms could no longer support her, her muscles trembling with the strain, she let go. She plunged into a snowbank, her skin shocked and freezing from the icy snow crystals enveloping her. So strong was the wind that it pressed the flimsy fabric of her nightdress tight against her bare skin and whipped long auburn strands of hair into her face.

She struggled to her feet, checking to see if her body still functioned. A quick perusal found nothing broken, though her foot dripped blood on the pure white snow from the puncture wound, bright drops that froze into diamond-shaped rubies visible in the reflected streetlamps pooling on the snowbanks. She shuddered.

The light was also exposing her body in stark relief for the killer.

Blood pounding in her ears and her breath ragged, she ran across the snow-covered yard to the neighbor's house some distance away. All the homes in the area were on five-acre allotments with everyone appreciating the privacy, but too far apart when help was required, like right now. Each footstep she took was an icy torment she had no choice but to ignore.

Please be home.

She stumbled through the line of tall trees that bordered each property, then the last few meters, her feet and legs wooden with the lack of sensation.

"Help! I need help! Let me in!" She pounded with both fists on the steel door, her chest heaving, cold sweat trickling down her sides. Shivering uncontrollably, she kept up the incessant knocking, barely registering the pain of flesh burning from the searing cold. *Please, please let someone be home.*

Precious seconds slipped by. Was that movement behind her? She spun around, her teeth chattering. Squinting into the darkness made her trembling increase, fueled by fresh terror, just as the frigid night made her bones ache. She could see nothing, her vision too blurry without her glasses to be certain her eyes weren't playing tricks. But she could hear him. Just like she had that fateful day hiding behind the false partition in her closet that her daddy had built for her, making her practice getting into the cramped space, over and over again. Hearing him breathing in the blackness, his evil intentions tainting the air.

He was coming for her. And this time her daddy wasn't there to protect her. She swallowed, her whole body shaking violently while her mind pictured the horror of what he intended to do to her. What he had done to her entire family...

Dear God, she prayed, *please, please let me in. Before it's too late.*

Chapter Four

Nick Wheeler slumped onto the sofa and breathed in the familiar scent of the fabric softener wafting from the chintz covers. He lurched forward and picked up the gold-edged photograph on the end-table, nearly overturning his glass of whiskey perched precariously on the glass top in the process.

A kaleidoscope of memories clicked by as he stared at the two smiling faces, each more heartbreaking than the last. His parents had shared so much. Their lives. Their laughter. And mostly a love that had enriched everyone they met. As lucky as they'd been in finding that one person that brought out the best in them, and made their lives ever better, his had turned out to be just the opposite. A string of women no more interested in hearth and home than a bloody zombie.

What was it his father had always said? *Yeah, happy wife, happy life. Maybe. But first you have to find someone who shares the same vision. The same standards and morals.* He snorted, grabbed his glass of whiskey and downed the last few gulps, holding on to the photo. He clasped it to his chest and sighed. Maybe it was time to quit thinking it was ever going to happen for him. Here he was, thirty-five years old and not a single possibility for anywhere near the fairy-tale life his parents had led.

His chin trembled slightly as he squeezed his eyes shut, suppressing the tears that threatened to overwhelm him. He hiccupped a few times then grabbed the bottle of Crown Royal and poured a few more ounces out of the half-empty container into the heavy-bottomed glass, trying his best not to spill the amber liquor. His mother had liked a clean house, though it had always been welcoming as well, and he didn't want to dishonor that memory.

He took a few more sips of the drink. It wasn't working. It didn't help to obliviate any of his pain. *Useless.* He placed the glass back with a bang, set the photograph carefully down on the table, then lay on the sofa and watched the room spin. This was the part he hated. But it was of short duration. A loud pounding on the front door jackknifed him into sitting right the fuck back up, head aching.

A light went on over her head and her breath rushed out in a gasp. *Hurry, hurry. There's no time to waste…*

A couple of seconds passed, then the red door swung open. Nirvana beckoned through the tunneled light shining from the entranceway. She pushed her way through, not waiting to see who had let her in. It didn't matter. Just so long as it wasn't him, the monster outside. The monster whose life she'd saved. And for what? So he could come after her all over again? And yet she knew no other choice had existed, if she didn't want to become like him. That would be a living death.

She stumbled up against a hard, warm body. She latched on to it with all she possessed, wrapping herself right around the unsuspecting person. *A hero.* The only beacon of hope in her dark world. She took a deep breath, the odor of bourbon and tobacco filling her lungs with its sharp sweetness. So familiar. Her daddy had smoked a pipe, enjoyed good-quality Canadian rye whiskey from Gimli, Manitoba. The pain of his loss hit again with the force of Thor's hammer. It crippled her. She continued clinging to the man. Even in her befuddlement, she recognized that the person was male, far too large to be female, too firm. Too powerful. A solid wall.

It registered then that it was not Jack Wheeler who held hers—it was a stranger's arms she had fallen into and was clutching at dementedly with grasping fingers, locked in place.

"Who are you?" she asked, her throaty voice unrecognizable. He didn't let her go even though she slackened her grip.

"I'm Nick. Nick Wheeler. But more importantly, who are you?" His voice was deep, resounding from his impossibly large chest. She tried to push away from him, realizing her breasts, naked under the nearly see-through nightgown, were pressed up tight against his firmness and that her nipples, budded from the cold, poked into him in a way that would be embarrassing on a normal day. But this was so far from a normal day that she couldn't even see back across the insane line she'd just crossed.

He defeated her actions, holding her tight and not letting her go. A cloud of alcohol fumes drifted around them, enticing on an elemental level. He had been drinking. Heavily. She looked into his face for the first time, liking what she saw, though fresh worry kept her tense. Had she jumped into the fire? *Maybe.* But this, this was a far different fire, a firestorm she would have embraced at another time, another place.

A chiseled jawline slightly obscured by five-o'clock shadow and dark fathomless eyes hooded by thick eyebrows greeted her minute study. He reminded her of a Roman gladiator. *A dangerous man. Warrior creed. Timeless.* Everything else slipped away, pushed to the furthest recesses of her brain while she continued to stare up at him, noting a crescent-shaped scar bisecting one black slash of an eyebrow.

Her perusal was returned with interest by a raw male spirit locking on to her now that her guard was down. His nostrils flared, breathing in her essence. The vision stirred her inner core to full wakefulness. And one simple fact. He was male to her female. A primal man. An answered call of truth and lust.

It defied everything she'd thought she knew about herself up until that precise second. A game changer. There was then, and there was now. Passion rose from deep inside her body to dance across the surface of her skin, making her aware of things she had never given any credence to before. It took her aback, hearing the distant siren's call coming closer and closer.

Why here? Why now? Her skin had become too sensitive, too needy, wanting something more that defied logic. Was she willing to make a trade for this harbor? Was that it? Was it just the basic instinct to succumb to the promise of safe passage in the whirlwind?

No.

She was in charge, making the present reach up and try to obscure the past, leave it behind. To forget for just one hour, one minute, one second the heavy baggage of her life. The troubles that few had seen, and hopefully fewer ever had to endure.

He reached up then with one hand that visibly trembled and placed it on her face. His rough fingertips skimmed over her cheeks, soothed back her wild hair, while his eyes searched her as if for the answers to the universe. She had none. Only questions.

"Who are you?" he asked, his voice raw from whiskey and smoke. The female he held in his arms, unable to let go, gave off the potent elixir of sex and fear. Her perfect body pressed to his own seduced and entranced him with its curves, hollows and soft skin. Lust consumed him even while danger signs loomed at every turn.

What the hell is going on?

He wished he hadn't drunk so much — his mind was slow to react, befuddled by intoxication. His body had a different approach to the situation. His cock was still hard from his recent dream, demanding and throbbing between his legs, making it difficult to focus on anything else. He had wanted to forget everything tonight, ease the pain, but now he was filled with regret. He should have set the liquor aside. But who could be prepared for this? This turn of events. This whirlwind of lust.

"Alysia Rossini. I — I live next door." Her voice held a sweetness mixed in with the stark fear. She was naked under the short babydoll nightie, still shivering. "Where're Jack and Susan?"

The pain hit hard, making it impossible to take a breath. *Breathe, just breathe.* Forcing down his anxiety and anger at the situation, he found his voice again.

"They're gone." His parents' deaths had woken the dragon—the pain he had tamped down for years after losing his only brother had now finally caught up with him.

She tried to pull away then, but he held on tighter, her trembling speaking to him on an elementary level that required no words. Her body was a beacon of light in the dark, a promise of comfort, one made to help him forget what was eating him alive. *Threatening to consume me.* And maybe, just maybe, she needed him as much as he needed her. He smelled it on her, the same sharp odor of desperation for something, *anything*, to help a person forget.

"Gone? Gone where?" Her voice held layers of panic, softening something inside him.

"I'm sorry. They were in an accident a few days ago. Head-on collision with a semi. They're gone—moved on to wherever good souls go." The stark words jabbed another shard of pain into him. *Why? How could this happen? One minute alive, the next dead?*

"Oh, my God, I'm so sorry. I hadn't heard anything about it," she said, her beautiful face tightening with concern. And it was a beautiful face even in distress. Classic bone structure with high, rounded cheeks and framed by masses of gorgeous auburn hair like a woman in a fairy tale. One slight flaw made her even more interesting—a tiny scar on her chin. But the most arresting part of her, beyond the curvy body he had no intention of letting go, were her intense green eyes that glittered even in the low light of the foyer. The woman of his dreams.

A loud thumping on the door once more sent his heart rate skyrocketing.

Alysia started in his arms, her striking eyes locking with his for a moment that near stopped his heart. He let her go and took up the Glock lying on the front hall table.

"Who is it?" he called, giving a quick gesture at Alysia to move away. She sprinted out of sight.

"Police," a sharp, formal voice declared.

Nick flattened his body against the wall and unlocked the door, then opened it slightly and peered out. A cop in uniform stood outside, an old, confused-looking man next to him. He sighed, put the Glock in the top drawer of the table and opened the door.

"Sorry to bother you so late at night, sir, but do you know this man?" the cop asked. Nick glanced at the befuddled man beside him, his dyed black hair in stark contrast to his wrinkled skin, and slicked back with the prominent widow's peak exposed. At least he was dressed warmly in a down parka, thick gloves and lined snow boots.

"Yes, he's my grandfather. His name's Walter."

"We found him wandering around Jasper Park," the cop said.

"Where's Susan?" Walter asked in a frail voice.

"Susan and Jack were in an accident a week ago. They're gone, I'm sorry, Pops." Nick forced the pain back down and turned back to the cop. "Walter, my grandfather, just moved in with them recently so it's hit him hard." He was here to clean up the mess, and his grandfather, such as he was, was his last remaining relative in the world.

The cop's expression turned solemn. "I'm very sorry for your loss. He was with some young men who took off when they spotted us. I think they might have been about to rob him. They're known drug dealers and petty criminals."

"Thank you for bringing him home, Officer."

"You should make sure he stays indoors," the cop said in a sharper tone. "Wandering around at three a.m. is dangerous. Anything could happen. Lucky we were there."

"You're right. I'll keep a better eye out." Nick ran a hand through his hair, knowing the cop could smell the booze on him.

"Okay then. I'll leave him in your custody. Good night."

The cop took his leave and Nick let out a huge sigh. He and his grandfather looked silently at each other for a few seconds, waiting for the cop to walk back down the sidewalk.

"God damn it, Walter," Nick exploded, not even bothering to look around to see if Alysia was in earshot. "What the hell was that all about?" His grandfather had been watching way too much of that TV show *Ray Donovan*, and thought the character played by John Voight was a good template for his own life. The Donovan patriarch had even pretended feebleness one episode to escape a prison sentence. *God damn it all to hell.* He could only pray that Walter didn't pick up the other bad habits of Mickey Donovan that were far worse than the womanizing and sleazy criminal enterprises.

"Seemed like the thing to do," Walter said, the confusion vanishing from his face in a split second. "You'd like me to get arrested, wouldn't you, so you could say 'I told you so'? Look at you, stinking of alcohol. Ha, what I do is no worse."

"Liquor is legal, unlike the shit you use. And what the hell were you doing out in the middle of the damn night?"

"Buying…a present for Cheriè, a babe I met at the Legion. I was doing her a solid—I need the comfort of a woman after this week. Surely you can understand that at least."

Nick shut his eyes and counted to ten. Yeah, he got it on one level. "How old is Cheriè?"

"A *very* spry seventy-one, if you know what I mean." Walter waggled his white eyebrows to further the point. "It was a little going-away present. A favor for a favor. Now it's all ruined thanks to a nosy cop. I was just doing a little standard transaction, like what happens on every street corner in North America every day. No harm in that."

"Walter, I'm only going to say this once. I swear, if you start this nonsense up again in Vancouver, I will put you in a home."

"Nick, my boy, at my age, a man should be able to do what he wants. You did get us a place with a hot tub, right? That's a chick magnet right there. And don't forget to call me Walter around the women. Grandpa spoils the mood."

Nick didn't trust himself to speak. His grandfather continued, "Now, I'm going to bed. I suggest you do the same. We've got a drive ahead of us tomorrow." He patted Nick's arm in a condescending manner and Nick counted to ten again. It didn't help. He still wanted to strangle someone.

Alysia chose that moment to walk back into the room. Walter gave a low whistle. "Good taste. Looks like it runs in the family, Nick-Nick. Say, you'd better do something about the lady's foot—it's bleeding."

Nick forgot all about his grandfather in looking down with horror at the bloodstained appendage. The woman's foot was dainty and tiny, like the rest of her. But how had he missed noticing that she was hurt? Unfortunately, he knew the why. His cock had been the one in charge. Time to rectify that.

"Come. We need to bandage your foot. And find you some warm clothing." Not that he wanted to cover up any of that gorgeous woman-flesh, but no way could he let his grandfather—the quintessential hound dog—prove more chivalrous than himself. Not even on his worst day was that remotely acceptable.

At least the surge of adrenaline had cleared away most of the lingering fog of alcohol and lust. He beckoned at his new guest hesitating in the doorway, giving her what he hoped was a reassuring smile. "I promise I don't bite. I leave that up to my grandfather and his con-of-the-day."

She snorted. "That was some show. I must remember that ruse. I may need it one day."

"Best not to hang around with Walter. He'll just get you into trouble."

She studied him with eyes pure as the deep waters in Green Lake, the vacation spot north of Whistler his parents had taken him and his brother Grayson to for the short, precious years of their childhood. The memory of loss hit again, cut him to the bone, the pain a constant raw loop that had been occurring all week long. He quickly hid it behind a façade of getting down to the business at hand of helping the woman who had turned up at his doorstep at three in the morning.

He pointed at the living room. "Have a seat. I'll get some bandages."

She turned and limped to the sofa. He grabbed an emergency kit from the drawer in the front hallway table — his parents had placed them all around the house, he'd discovered — and carried it back to her side. He sat on the ottoman in front of her and she trembled slightly. His heart squeezed in sympathy.

Reaching up behind her, he pulled the colorful rainbow-striped afghan his mother had crocheted off the back of the sofa, tucking it in around her body. The actions brought him into close proximity to her and he again was treated to the fragrance of arousal wafting off her. Her sexual aura was undeniable. It reached out and grabbed him around the throat and other parts farther south.

"Thanks," she said. She gave a wince of pain when he picked up her foot to inspect it. The riot of color from the handmade throw around her body added a sense of knowing her, because he had an identical one at his place.

"Have you had a recent tetanus shot?"

"Yes, one of the hazards of the business." She chewed on her bottom lip, watching him dab at the wound with some iodine then apply a plastic bandage.

"What business is that?"

"I work as a trauma nurse for BC-STAR."

He raised his eyebrows in appreciation. "Oh. You're one of the people who get to ride around in helicopters to accident scenes."

"Yes. We go to some pretty brutal accidents."

"I'm sorry. I should have realized that. I can only imagine what you've seen — been exposed to." He gave her a direct look. Her eyes locked with his. He swallowed. *Hard.* The lust still simmered under the surface — for both of them. "What happened tonight?"

She shook her head, her lips pressed together in a tight line. Her throat moved up and down, a pulse beating too rapidly at the delicate base of her neck. Exactly where he'd like to start kissing her. The perfect spot to taste her. His vision dropped lower to the deep V of her breasts exposed by the drape of the blanket. He swallowed again, barely able to keep from reaching out to touch her, to experience again the heat of her. The memory was seared into his body and brain.

He looked up again, right into her eyes. Those all-knowing eyes. He flushed, exposed.

"Do we need to call the cops?" he asked. It was kind of late, and they'd already been here once tonight and she hadn't stepped forward to say anything. In hindsight, that was strange. Plus, she could have called nine-one-one at any time on her cell phone. He must have been too spaced-out by the drink to catch that. Of course, he'd had his grandfather's exploits hampering him.

"No. They didn't believe me before, why would they now?"

Her words startled him as their meaning sank in.

"This has happened before? And what exactly did happen tonight?" His professional shell clicked into place. Now he was all business.

She chewed on her bottom lip, the lines of her lovely face expressing concern.

"I'm not the enemy here. I can help you, if you can't go to the police." He stepped out on a limb with the words. What if she was one of the bad guys and not one of the innocent victims his TETRAD group would want to help? But something told him this woman was the real deal. She was fleeing something horrible and she needed him. He could never turn his back on that situation, however it played out.

"I think he's in my house," she said in a hushed tone, as though afraid of being overheard. She leaned her head forward, her hair moving to veil her face. What had happened to bring such a strong woman to her knees? No one who couldn't pull their own weight was part of the BC-STAR group.

"Who's in your house?" he pressed. He reached toward her and tucked a thick curl of her auburn hair behind her ear in efforts to better see her face.

"The man who murdered my family." She looked into his eyes, saying the horrific words in a deadened tone of voice. Words that no one should ever have to speak, let alone live through. Stunned, he could only stare back and see the truth of it in green eyes swimming with unshed tears. *My God, it was real. That nightmare really happened. To this beautiful woman.*

He jumped up. "Stay here," he commanded, his tone sharp.

"No! Don't go. He's evil—he'll kill you," she begged, trying to grasp at his arm.

"No, he won't." And, with that reassurance, he hurried back to the front hallway to retrieve his gun and overcoat.

"Stop! Hold on! I think I smelled—"

Chapter Five

Too late, he was already out of the front door. Alysia scrambled up from the sofa and limped across the hardwood floor, prepared to follow him into hell if that was what it took. She had to warn him.

Thrusting open the hall closet bi-fold door, she searched for a pair of shoes — any kind. A pair of small woman's winter boots sat primly together right beside a much larger pair that appeared masculine in nature. Overlooking the fact that they most likely belonged to a dead woman, she tugged them onto her bare feet. Above the footwear hung a few coats, enough to cover weather in all seasons. Ignoring them, she drew the afghan closer about her shoulders.

She raced into the freezing night, not giving herself a second to think about what she was doing in running toward a madman. She'd never be able to bring herself to do it if she gave it any thought.

What had his grandfather called him? Nick-Nick. Obviously a play on his name. *Yeah, like Ray-Ray. Cute, when you're five.*

"Nick!" she screamed at the top of her lungs, running full speed across the yard. She hit the border of trees between the properties and slowed down a bit to navigate around the huge tree trunks.

KABOOM.

The reverberations of the explosion wiped away her balance in an instant. She fell to her knees in the deep snow, bile rising into her throat, her ears ringing loudly.

She forced herself to her feet. "Nick! Where are you, Nick?" she shouted, the cold, moist air rushing into her lungs, heavy with ice and dread. *My God, if he's hurt because of all this when he just wanted to help me –*

She might have just met Nick, but she saw something special in him. A man who was going through the minefield of the recent loss of his parents. His pain and grief spoke to her on the most basic of levels.

So help me, God, as you are my witness, I will avenge Nick if he's hurt because of me. I will kick that murderous asshole into a dark hole he'll never escape from. She totally regretted her soft heart when she'd had the chance to end the life of a monster. Right now, at this moment, the outcome of that fateful night would be far different if she was offered the chance again.

She zigzagged through the snow on shaky limbs barely able to support her, floundering and falling to her knees a couple of times in the deep piles. Not having her glasses to correct her short-sightedness drove her near insane. *Where is he?* She tripped and fell, landing hard, having fallen over something half-hidden in the snow. Untangling her limbs, she scrambled to her feet, ready to run.

"Don't go, it's me, Nick," he said, his voice harsh and gravelly.

"Nick!" She dropped and crouched by his side. "Are you okay? Are you hurt?"

"I'm fine. Just got tossed by the explosion is all. Pretty sure nothing's broken." He rolled over and lumbered to his feet, swaying a bit. He offered his hand. She grasped it and he pulled her to her feet.

"Oh, thank God!" She threw herself into his arms, hugging him tight. The throw fell from her shoulders and pooled on the ground, forgotten.

He hugged her back just as tightly. It felt like they'd known each other their whole lives instead of just one night.

Chapter Six

Nick crushed Alysia to his body, his mind filled with the horror at what could have happened. If she hadn't gotten away, run to him, if she'd been overcome by the propane that must have been filling the house even as she slept, she'd have been blown up. This beautiful, vital woman would no longer be here in his arms. *Alive.* His protection instinct filled him with righteous anger. How could this have happened? How had a madman been operating under their very noses? And right next door, the final insult.

"Did you see him?" she asked.

No need to say whom. That was a given.

"No, I saw nothing. He must have made his escape. Or maybe we got lucky and he blew himself up along with your house. I'm sorry. Maybe if I'd asked you sooner what was going on, we could have saved your home."

She shook her head, nestled in under his chin in an effort to keep warm. He liked having her there, loved the naturalness to it that defied everything that normally went into meeting a woman. They'd skipped about a dozen steps, but he wasn't complaining.

"It goes as it's meant to, Nick. Sooner might just have guaranteed getting hurt if we'd entered the house."

"True. Oh fuck, I just realized all your stuff is gone. Come, I'll call the fire department if the neighbors haven't already, and find you something to wear."

He reached down and picked up the abandoned throw, tucking it around her shoulders before escorting her back to his parents' house. Or what used to be his parents' home. The realization hit him afresh, making him squeeze Alysia even tighter against his side. She didn't pull away in protest, just tried matching his strides across the snowy reaches of the vast yard. He slowed down to make it easier for her.

Faint sirens in the distance alerted him to incoming. He increased his speed again, helping Alysia to hurry and get inside the front door. He found his grandfather, disheveled and glassy-eyed, standing in the front entrance, gun in hand.

"What the hell happened?" Walter asked, his eyes as round as an owl's.

"Give me the gun and we'll tell you," Nick said, reaching out a hand to take the weapon from the old man. Walter handed it over after a slight pause. He watched his grandson slip it into the pocket of his overcoat.

"Why ya hanging on to it?"

"Been some developments."

"Yeah? What kind of developments? Her husband coming after you both?"

Horrified, Nick took a deep breath. The last thing he needed was that kind of rumor getting started, especially with the fire department and the cops on their way.

"I'm not married. And no, I just met your grandson tonight, so nothing's going on between us," Alysia said. Her tone was cool, as though the comments hadn't raised her blood pressure, unlike himself. Though he was pleased to hear about her unmarried status.

"Could have fooled me," Walter said, pursing his lips and rolling his eyes.

"Listen, I'm only going to say this once. Alysia showed up here after discovering a man had broken into her house in the middle of the night. She ran over here for our help. And the perp must have turned on the propane, setting the place on fire. Got it?"

"Cheez, yeah, I got it. You don't have to be so damn self-righteous about it. I get it—you're not tapping that ass. Your loss."

"Walter, so help me—"

Gales of laughter broke through his anger. He spun around to see Alysia holding her sides, tears streaming down her cheeks. Her pale face suggested she'd reached the end of her tolerance for stress tonight.

"Walter, pour her a drink. I'll sit her down." Nick took her arm and led her over to the sofa, covering her up.

Walter did what he was asked for once and hurried back with a half-full tumbler of whiskey.

"Here, drink some of this."

She dutifully took the glass and swallowed a bit. Then took a few gulps, handing it back nearly empty. "Thanks, I needed that."

"I like to see a woman who can hold her liquor," Walter said with approval. "If she'll take out the garbage, marry her."

"Just ignore him. He'll go away if he knows what's good for him."

She smiled at him, her first genuine smile. It was earth-shattering, as if the heavens opened and an angel appeared. A smile that could light up a room, or a man's heart. He shook his head. What in hell was wrong with him tonight? *Must be in shock from a slight concussion.* But no time to get that checked — he had a new case to solve.

"Do you have something I could put on?"

"Sure. Walter, could you please grab something for Alysia to wear? Thank you."

The old man left the room, grumbling about being a damn slave to the man.

"We don't have much time, so we need to get our stories straight. What do you want to tell the police?"

"Nothing. Absolutely nothing about anyone being in the house. It will be chalked up to a propane leak, most likely. The man who did this, he's very, very clever — genius IQ — and he'd leave no evidence of his ever having been there. You can be absolutely certain of that. I just can't go there again. Please, if nothing else, you've *got* to believe me when I say the police will only make things worse. There's so much you don't know. How much he will make everyone suffer. Poe is absolute evil. *Please*, *please*, I beg you." Her tone was the plea of a desperate person. It hit him hard, made him rethink what direction to take.

"Fine, but only if you let me help you. I belong to a group of people who help those that can't call upon the law for help. We call ourselves TETRAD. And we're the guys you come to when there's nowhere else to turn. We have a different mix of abilities and skills to bring to the cause. Mine happens to be criminal profiling, negotiations and weaponry."

"TETRAD. You'd do that? Help out a virtual stranger?"

"Of course. We're sworn to help those who most need it. Looking at how this situation has you in such a state, I think you need it as much or more than anyone I've ever met. Please, let us help you."

She chewed on her bottom lip, staring into deep space before turning and looking him in the eyes. The clearness of her vision was a direct hit to his solar plexus, made him want to help her any way humanly possible. "I don't have that much money saved up, but I promise to pay you, however long it takes." She hesitated, waving away his protest that he didn't expect any money with a hand gesture. "But I'm not so certain you should get involved. That man—he's a monster. I think what a profiler like you would call an organized serial killer. He got away with it once when he was at university. He'll be even more prepared this time round."

"I don't care how prepared he is, how organized he is, or how fucking brilliant he is. He's going down. You have my solemn word on it."

He took her chilly hands in his and rubbed them between his own to warm them, finding them to be strong and yet dainty. *Just like the rest of her.* She continued locking eyes with him, as if searching for something. Finally, she spoke. "I believe you."

Her words filled him with confidence accompanied by an immediate inpouring of strength and vitality. Even his fucking headache from the explosion abated.

He cleared his throat. "Good. Tomorrow we head into Vancouver and get the team onboard."

"Vancouver? Ahh—okay. But I will need to stop by BC-STAR first, pick up a few things from my locker and talk to my supervisor about getting some time off."

Walter came back into the room, drawing their attention. "I found this. Will it work?" He held up a Vancouver Canucks sweatshirt, a pair of boxer briefs and a long, bulky denim skirt.

"Perfect, thank you, Walter." Alysia got up and kissed the old man on both cheeks in the old-fashioned way.

"Anything for such a pretty lady," he said, grinning ear to ear. Nick was chagrined by the stab of jealousy. She hadn't even kissed him yet. And thanking the man for such a ridiculous costume defied explanation. Now, a short, tight red dress—that would set fire to the world. *Hmm.* Bad choice of phrasing, but it got him back on track and not daydreaming about all that womanly flesh. *Maybe.*

He cleared his throat. "You can change in the bathroom down the hall. First door on your right."

The sirens were insistently announcing their presence now, flashes of red light glowing through the draped front picture window.

"Okay, Walter. I need you to have my back on this."

"You don't have to say anything. I'm not deaf. No way would I'd tell those coppers anything. At least you don't work for *them.*"

Coming from Walter, that was almost a compliment.

Chapter Seven

Alysia closed the bathroom door. She laid the clothing and her phone on top of the hamper then turned on the taps over the basin of the sink. She scooped her hands together and splashed the warm water all over her face, using her wet fingers to rake her thick hair back. She stared at her reflection in the medicine cabinet mirror, allowing the drops to drip off her chin and onto her chest.

Cool, assessing eyes stared back at her. He'd taken from her all over again. Even after she'd saved his damn life, he had to come back, to take even more. A home she'd spent years getting the way she wanted it. *You fucking bastard.* Bile rose in her aching throat. She clenched the edge of the sink, rocking back and forth, trying to ease her pain and grief.

Her eyes filled with tears she angrily shook away. No way would she let him win this time. No. This time she had help. Nick and his crew were going to have her back. What had he called them? Yeah, TETRAD. He'd promised her, and it was clear he was a man of his word. She just hoped she hadn't just put more people in danger. But she had a good feeling about him. Nick was a strong man, a man used to working outside the law. He had a skillset that regular guys did not. And, most important, he had courage. He'd run into danger, not away.

They were kindred spirits. She constantly ran toward trouble as well—which was probably why, in her downtime, like most on her trauma crew, she turned to alcohol, sex or drugs. Sometimes all three at the same time when away at a convention, now that marijuana was legal in Canada. Not that she considered herself a slut. She chose her partners carefully, practiced safe sex, always making sure they weren't interested in a long-term relationship. No one was safe around her. And everyone she knew played hard and worked harder, trying their best to forget what they experienced attending to broken and damaged human bodies on a daily basis.

Alysia finished drying her face. She removed her nightgown and hung it on a metal hook behind the bathroom door, then yanked on the clothes Walter had provided. Except for the lack of a bra, which the jersey couldn't totally hide, the outfit worked in a good way and covered her from head to toe. She'd need the sense of security and control, heading into this fray. Circumventing questions with the law was never an easy task. But what had they ever done for her?

She straightened her shoulders, tucking her hair behind her ears and sighing out loud. What she wouldn't give for a headband or hair tie and her glasses. *Hmm.* Nick had a bottle of whiskey she'd be willing to share to make this god-awful night go away.

Or maybe not. It was just a few hours till dawn and tomorrow promised to be tough enough without a bloody hangover.

She exited the bathroom as ready as she was ever going to be. Exhaustion threatened and darkened the edges of her vision, tunneled it, making her sway a bit on the way down the hallway, the long skirt whispering as it brushed the floor. *Hang in there, you can rest soon, sweetheart.* The voice of her father gave her bittersweet strength and she forced herself to put one foot in front of the other.

A loud knock on the front door alerted her to the expected visitors. She glanced at Nick and his grandfather, letting them know with a quick hand gesture that she had herself together. Sort of true. Nick gave her a reassuring look in return, then went to let them in. *Showtime.*

Two RCMP officers entered on a rush of frosted air, giving the three of them a quick appraisal. She stood tall, grateful the skirt was long enough to cover her bare feet. Had her truck been damaged in the explosion? If not, she kept a pair of spare glasses and her portable trauma kit inside. *Damn it.* The bag in the vehicle held the tools of her nursing profession, the ones she'd used on the highway that fateful night, and the very ones she'd used to help the man who had tried to take her life yet again.

"Evening, or should I say morning," the taller of the officers said, making a small joke. "Sorry to bother you, but we're looking for the woman who lives next door. Would that be you, ma'am?"

"I'm Alysia Rossini, and I own the house." Alysia gave a shudder along with the words of acknowledgment.

"Were you there tonight when the event happened?"

She'd already given this a bit of thought, a way to explain why she wasn't in bed and hadn't been blown up along with the house. She gave the officers her best doe-eyed expression. "Yes, but I was lucky. Oh, boy, was I lucky! I had just stepped out for a cigarette when the explosion happened. I was thrown to the ground, then I ran over here for help and fortunately Nick was home. He let me in. Must have been a gas leak or something like that. Right?"

"Do you always step outside in twenty below weather to have a cigarette?" he asked, his glance her way a bit more intense, his eyes narrowing.

"I have a close friend, Kate. She's dying of lung cancer and she's very sensitive to smoke. I never smoke in the house."

"Of course. I'm sorry to hear about your friend," he said, appearing satisfied with her answer. "I'm afraid there's not much left of your house. I hope you have insurance?"

She bit down on her bottom lip. "Yes, I do."

"The cause of the fire will be determined by an investigator within the fire department. If it indeed turns out to be an accident, your insurance should allow you to rebuild."

She ignored his suggestion that it might turn out to be arson. "What about my truck? It was parked in the garage out back — behind the house. Is it still standing?"

"I don't know that, Miss Rossini. You'll have to check with someone on scene. The fire department's still working on it, but they have it under control." The officer looked at Nick. "Did you hear or see anything, sir?"

"I heard the explosion. I was here—in the house. I'd had a few drinks." Nick scrubbed a hand down his face. "Been a tough week. My parents were killed this week in a highway accident. My grandfather here, Walter" — he nodded toward the old man—"was in bed at the time. The explosion woke him up."

She bit her lip, watching the flash of pain pass over his face when he mentioned his parents.

"Sorry for your loss, sir. Well, if you think of anything else, please give us a call." He gave her a business card and handed one to Nick.

The officers took their leave, the equipment attached to their leather belts thumping and jolting against their Kevlar vests, and their heavy-soled boots squeaking on the hardwood floor. Nick stepped up and locked the door behind them. The sounds of the deadbolt clicking into place changed the dynamics of the room in an instant. *Cocooned. And safe from prying eyes.* She let out a deep breath. *One problem averted.*

"I need a drink. Join me?" He turned and gave her a direct stare, his question more a gauntlet thrown down than an invitation. His confident manner suggested she would say yes to him. It only added to his allure. A vision of having been in his arms on that very spot an hour ago, pressed up against all that hot man-flesh, breathing in the intoxicating scent of mutual arousal— everything combined to send goosebumps coursing up and down her body.

She hugged her arms tight around herself, her eyelids half-closed and her breathing shallow while she licked her bottom lip. She wanted to taste him, discover if he would be as good in bed as he looked. She was a woman entirely sure of her sexuality. Why not? She'd seen firsthand how precious and fleeting human existence was. It could be snuffed out from one soft breath to the next. *So grab pleasure when it's offered.* She licked her lips again and looked him up and down, signaling her intentions.

"I'll have one," Walter said.

"You're not invited. I need to speak with Alysia alone. Now."

"That's the thanks I get! Cheez, I should have told those coppers the real deal. That little missy here showed up well before the explosion. Looks to know who did it, too. And that my grandson is involved in it up to his eyeballs."

"Take the opened bottle, Walter. And good night." Nick didn't appear too worried about his grandfather's threats. Besides, she didn't see Walter as the kind of guy who'd go babbling to the police. Not after what she had heard earlier about his exploits in the park. He was no righteous tattletale. He couldn't afford to be.

"Nice howdy-do when a man has to drink alone," Walter said. But he took off at a fast clip for an old guy, snatching the half-empty whiskey bottle with one hand right off the living room side table and exiting down the hallway still muttering to himself, shoes scuffling the floor. A door slammed at the back of the house. They were alone. *Finally.*

She walked over to join Nick, standing close to him by the living room bar that was nothing more than an assortment of liquors and a few glasses around an ice bucket on a side table. She watched as he opened a new bottle of twenty-five-year-old rye, listening to the soft *glug-glug* as he poured three fingers' worth into two heavy-bottomed crystal glasses.

She took the glass from his outstretched hand, letting her fingers drift along his warm flesh. He looked her in the eyes then, watching while she took a deep, appreciative swallow of the excellent whiskey without breaking visual contact, enjoying the light, sensuous burn as it flowed down the back of her throat and warmed her body.

"Do you want to take a look at your place or sit and talk first?" he asked. "There's so much I need to know about this situation. So much planning — "

"No talking. And I certainly don't want to see the smoldering ruins of my former house. What's behind door number three?"

Much as he wanted to lay her down and have his way with her then and there, it wasn't right. He had to protect her, even if it was from herself, because the invitation was clear in her body language, in her amazing eyes, in the fragrance of pheromones sharpening the air with the essence of arousal.

"You've been through a lot tonight. I don't think — "

She put a finger to his lips. "Don't think or talk. Just let yourself feel, Nick, let yourself go. It's the only way."

Oh My God, but she made it hard. Knowing what was under that silly costume, the hot incredible warmth of her. What man in his right mind would turn her down? He'd be certifiable.

She set her half-empty glass down and cradled his face with her hands. Her touch made something deep inside him stir while his cock firmed and lengthened. One part of him was more than certain that this was the best idea yet.

"You are so damn fine," she murmured. She slipped her hands behind his neck while he struggled to hold himself together. She tugged on his hair, drawing him down to her. Pressed her oh-so-soft lips against his, her hot breath slipping into him, fragrant with the potent whiskey.

"You taste so fucking good," she said, pushing her tongue inside his mouth to tangle with his. She sucked on his tongue, suggesting how well she could perform on other body parts, pressing her lush mouth tight against his, her unrestrained breasts full and swollen against his chest. Her nipples budded, thrusting into his flesh.

Christ, give me the strength to do the right thing.

But he had to have a full taste first, fisting his hands in her glorious mane and pulling her in tighter, letting her feel the full length of him. God, how he wanted her. But no, it wasn't right. The timing was all wrong. An adrenaline surge blew through him again. So much he needed to find out, too. So much he needed to know.

"No," he said, pulling her away from him, his hands still clenched in her hair. "I can't do that to you. You're vulnerable right now. Not thinking straight. I want it to be right between us." And only after he had made her safe should he cross that line.

She pulled back, her lips pursed together in a pout. "Fine. If you don't want me, just say so. Don't make up some rubbish about it not being right. I'm well beyond the age of majority."

"My God, do you know how much I want to just *fuck* you right now?" His frustration boiled over, making him curse. This simmering cauldron of finding this amazing woman in his house, a woman pursued by a killer who'd murdered her family, then having the same monster come and set her home on fire. It was a quagmire to his baser instincts. And the worst part was that he was teetering on the edge of accepting. To just letting go and forgetting. To being inside this glorious woman. He wanted to kiss her. Taste her. Fuck her every way imaginable—no holds barred.

She bit her lip and took up her glass again, finishing the remaining liquor.

"Where do I sleep?"

With me. Instead, he cleared his throat. "There's a spare room." He swallowed the last of his drink. The potent elixir soothed his jangling nerves. He stood taller, pissed that he'd given the game away, let her know how much he wanted her. But she already did know—he saw it reflected back at him in her eyes. Saw it along with disappointment that scorched and tortured.

Chapter Eight

Day Two

"I apologize in advance for having to ask you some difficult things to get a clear idea of the perp and what he's capable of. You've shared that he's of above average intelligence, that he escaped prosecution because of his air-tight alibi and that the police dismissed your concerns as unfounded. Why do you think he's the guy?" Nick asked, setting his coffee down on the counter that separated the dining area from the kitchen.

Alysia sat cradling a hot cup of black coffee between her hands on a stool in the incongruously cheerful kitchen after a fitful few hours of sleep and a hot shower, wearing the same clothes from the night before. What did it matter what she wore? Nick sat beside her, his casual demeanor helpful in the face of what she had to share now, the whole painful truth.

Still, it rankled that she had to convince him that she knew the killer.

"My father and Edward Poe went into business together when I was a kid." Alysia rubbed her aching forehead, memories flooding in. "Our families spent a lot of time together, picnics, ball games, holidays, you name it. It was good, at first. Then my mom started saying I should stay clear of their son, that I should never be alone with him. She wouldn't say why. But I'd heard rumors. That…that stuff went on with him and the other neighborhood children. He was sent away to private school quite young. We hardly saw him after that except at Christmas and Easter."

"This asshole have a name?"

Alysia bit her lip, drawing blood, her voice shaky. "Jeffrey Poe."

"More coffee?"

She cleared her throat, the lump tightening inside making it difficult to breathe. "Sure, if you add a dram of whiskey." She held out her cup and Nick took it. He went over to the coffee machine, refilling hers and his with the steaming brew. He opened a kitchen cupboard and pulled out a bottle of whiskey, adding a full measure to each. As he brought it back to her, he sat beside her again.

"Go on," he urged. His professionalism was helping. She took a large gulp of the doctored drink and found the strength to continue.

"There was a falling out between my dad and his partner over missing money. It was later found to be the bookkeeper who had stolen it, but Edward blamed my dad for the business going belly up. He took to drinking heavily and one dark night he ran head-on into the path of a train, half-drunk and high. The collision killed him instantly, still thinking my dad had swindled him. There was talk it was suicide, but who knows."

She shrugged, the pain sluicing through her at the terrible tragedy that could have been prevented. "Then his mother, Helen, committed suicide with a drug overdose. Left a note about not being able to go on. And Jeffrey was left all alone. I guess he stewed in his anger after losing his family, blamed ours entirely for everything that had happened to him—" She stopped abruptly, her body trembling at knowing what she must reveal next. The worst thing of all. *Just state the facts. You can do it, sweetheart.* Her father's voice gave her strength.

"He came after us. He must have planned it really well because the police said he'd been seen at university that night by two other students who could verify his whereabouts."

"I'm apologizing in advance for this, but are you sure they were lying?"

She bit down on her inner cheek until she tasted blood. The reminder of the dismissal of her absolute certainty by other law enforcement still hurt to the core.

"Jeffrey has very unusual eyes. One blue, one brown. They stare right through you like you don't exist except for his amusement." She shuddered. "Impossible to miss. The cops even blamed me—said I must be seeing things or, worse, wanted to implicate our neighbor because of the old family feud over business dealings."

"So, his alibis must have been paid for or coerced via some kind of blackmail. How else could he escape justice?"

"You're a profiler. How does it work? What can you see?" Stalling into technicalities seemed a safer bet, dreading what she must still reveal.

"This case is different from my usual cases. We know the perp up front. Normally, I piece together a profile of who the criminal is. His crime scene actions help a great deal in understanding how his mind works. Linkage analysis, we call it, when we can connect it to any of his other crimes. Of course, his mood at the moment of the altercation can affect what he does or doesn't do."

"Cold rage. That's what I saw. He was fueled by it," she volunteered, shuddering again. She took a large gulp of the coffee to warm herself.

"It's unusual for such a young person to have done such pre-planning. It doesn't bode well."

"What do you mean?"

"Criminals get better at what they do—a pattern of progression. They live in a world of fantasy, going over and over what they're planning until it becomes a part of them. It becomes like a stage play to them."

She set her cup down, disheartened. "If he could plan such a terrible crime when he was so young, what is he capable of now?" Then a terrifying thought lurched into her mind. *"Oh my God*, do you think he's done something similar since?"

"Hard to say. But it's entirely possible. Or maybe he commits other kinds of crimes that satisfy his sick urges."

The horrifying thoughts hung between them.

"You know, I had the opportunity to let him die." The words spilled out as she explained what had happened that fateful night on the side of the icy road.

Nick didn't interrupt, just let her lay out all the facts in her own time.

"I don't know if I would do it the same way again," she said, looking him in the eyes, searching. What would he think of her now?

"But you didn't, so you'll never know. But my best guess, from what little I know about you, is that the outcome would remain the same. I wouldn't give it any more thought. No point. You're just torturing yourself."

She shrugged. "I don't know anymore. I think he wants to destroy me."

"Don't let him." Nick reached out and placed a large hand over hers, squeezing it gently.

"That's something my dad would have said. But it's not so easy."

"How did you escape that night?" His question caught her off guard. "I know this is hard. But best to get it all out now. It might even be cathartic for you."

Tears escaped and she angrily brushed them away. "I hid. My dad must have suspected something was coming—I don't know—but he made me practice hiding in a false wall in my closet. It had a built-in peephole that was invisible from the outside. Hidden in a crack between the cedar slats that he'd lined it with, I saw him come right into it, throwing my clothes to the floor, searching for me." More tears fell, blurring her vision.

"I'm so sorry, Alysia. I'm amazed by you."

That surprised her and she looked him in the eyes again, but saw only calm approval. "What do you mean?"

"You're so strong. You're here. You're a survivor."

"I don't know. I don't feel strong most of the time. I just feel numb." But even as she said it, she realized that wasn't quite right. A mishmash of emotions had arisen in the last twelve hours that hurt like hell. And underneath that, something else stirred, chipping away at the frozen block she'd become — a realization that she wanted to fight back even harder. To live authentically. To find her true self again, not exist like a damn robot like she'd been doing these past years. The old Alysia who loved life — did she even exist anymore?

"Well, you impress the hell out of me. You went on to work as a trauma nurse, not an easy job."

"I wanted to help others that have been hurt, so often through no fault of their own."

"More coffee?" he asked. She startled at some scuffling noises coming from the hallway just before someone entered the kitchen. Walter, wearing slippers, sweatpants and a T-shirt. She tugged her hand out from under Nick's, self-conscious at his grandfather being there.

"Mornin'," he said, shuffling toward the counter that housed the coffee machine. When he caught sight of her, he sucked in his pot belly with an infectious grin.

They both watched Walter pour himself a cup of coffee, then head to the refrigerator for a container of half and half. He added a liberal dose of the cream, stirred in two heaping teaspoons of sugar and drank a bit, smacking his lips in approval. "You make a fine cup of coffee, Nick-Nick. Almost as good as a Timmy's double-double. So — what's the deal today? We headed to Vancouver or not? I need to line up my ducks, or duckies" — he waggled his gray eyebrows in mock salute — "if you get my drift, if we're hanging around here. A man has his needs."

"Yes, we're going. But first I need to drive Alysia to her workplace to gather her things and make arrangements."

"No, you don't need to do that. I can drive myself, if my truck's still functioning," she said in protest.

"Not going to happen. From now on, I'm not letting you out of my sight, beautiful."

The word *beautiful* softened his uber-firm authoritative tone, while the meaning of his words grated. She hated being given an ultimatum by anyone, let alone a man she'd just met. But he had taken her in — that had to count for something. He was perhaps endangering himself by helping her. She took a deep breath.

"Okay." She glanced at the clock over the sink. "I'd like to check out my place now if that's okay?" She didn't want to — probably the last thing on earth she wanted to see was her home burned to the ground — but she had to know. Was there anything left?

"You should eat first. Going to be a challenging enough day as it is." Nick got up without waiting for her answer and strode over to the fridge, yanking the door handle open, reaching in and coming back with his hands full. He laid the carton of eggs on the counter alongside two tomatoes and bread and butter. A part of her liked being taken care of, but another part disliked it. She'd done for herself for years now and was perfectly capable of handling things on her own. But he was right, her stomach was empty, sloshing away from all the coffee, and the whiskey had just made her hungrier. She needed fortification.

"What can I do?" she asked, getting up to join him.

"I'll make the eggs. You can slice the tomatoes and toast the bread."

The hominess of the situation soothed her nerves as, watched by a coffee-drinking Walter, they both moved around the kitchen in tandem, occasionally bumping hips. The fragrance of eggs frying in butter and bread toasting raised her spirits.

Nick plated the eggs, she added the toast and they sat at the table, joining Walter. His grandfather reached out, surprising her by taking her hand, then his grandson's.

"Rub-a-dub-dub, bless this grub," he said.

"Walter," Nick said. Though he scrunched up his forehead, she caught a glimpse of a twinkle in his eyes. *Nice.*

"What? If it's good enough for Dirty Harry, good enough for me. You know, I could use a little walking-around money today, since our trip's being delayed."

Nick let out an exasperated breath. "What happened to the two hundred I gave you yesterday?"

Walter shrugged, swiped up the last of his yolk with a bit of toast and popped it in his mouth. "What can I say? Cheriè's an expensive bit of muff."

Alysia choked. Nick patted her back and his touch sent thrills racing up and down her spine.

"You okay?" he asked.

She nodded, not trusting herself to speak.

"We need to talk, Walter. NOW." Nick thrust his plate away and the legs of his chair skidded on the floor as he jerked his body backward. He got up from the table and marched out of the room, his boots echoing on the tile floor. Walter gave her a look of *what's his problem?* before standing and following his grandson.

Alysia got to her feet and collected the three empty plates and the silverware. She rinsed them in the sink before tucking them in the dishwasher. It was hard not to overhear the heated words resounding in the hallway between the generations. She shook her head. Walter, bless his devious heart, was a distraction from her worries.

Nick's grandfather's voice came through loud and clear. "What the fuck's the point of being old if you don't get to say what you damn well want!"

She couldn't hear Nick's responses but they sounded much more measured. Then the sounds of conversation died away completely.

When she was finished with her task, she strode to the window and crossed her arms over her chest, looking out on the backyard. She was unable to see her house from the limited view, but in her mind's eye she had a pretty good idea of the devastation that awaited. Bile rose in her throat and she swallowed it down. She needed to keep the sustenance onboard. *No time to be weak.*

Nick came back into the room alone, his expression harried.

"You know, it's okay, right?" She took a moment to reassure him. What did an old man's comments matter in the scheme of things? And laughs were hard to come by in her world. "I think your grandfather's funny. And a bit of humor can't hurt right now."

"I don't want him turning women into objects. I want him treating you with respect." Nick ran his hands through his hair.

She had nothing to say to that. She got that his heart was in the right place. She took a closer look at him, realizing that she'd not really taken in the details of his appearance with all that had happened. The sunlight streaming in the kitchen windows reflected off his burnished hair. It was a lion's mane of various shades of golden brown and blond, brushing his collar and contrasting with his Romanesque features. But his eyes were the most arresting part of him. Large for a man, expressive and whiskey-brown in color. He did resemble his parents. He had his father's face shape and his mother's eyes. Good family genetics.

She closed her eyes as a tidal wave of grief rushed over her. *So hard to believe that the Wheelers are gone. Such a loving, happy couple. And always together. The epitome of a couple still in love after decades of marriage. Will I ever have that?* If she were a betting woman, she'd lay heavy odds against it.

Chapter Nine

"Are you ready?" Nick asked, ignoring her generous comments about his grandfather.

"Yeah," she said, her expression tight. "Might as well get this over with."

He took a closer look at her. "You're welcome to anything in my mother's closet. Would you like to change before we go?"

"No, I'm fine. I have a change of clothes at work. And in my truck, if it's not been burned all to hell." He watched her swallow, the slender column of her throat moving, her face pale. So delicate, yet so strong. She intrigued him on every level. She even managed to look beautiful in the ludicrous outfit—he could only image how she'd look in proper-fitting clothes. Or, better yet, none at all. *Crap. Get your mind out of the gutter, Wheeler.* This day was going to be tough enough as it was. He needed to be there for her, support her.

He cleared his throat. "Okay. Let's head out of the front. We can grab you a winter coat from the closet there."

She nodded and he led the way.

He helped her into a parka his mother had seldom worn, then waited while she pulled on snow boots. He grabbed his gun and jacket, thrust his feet into his heavy winter boots and opened the front door. A bracing wind lashed his face, making him hope the sunshine would hold at least until they reached Vancouver. The last thing they needed was another winter storm. He scanned the street, looking for unusual activity, but all appeared normal and quiet. He'd have to be on guard twenty-four-seven from now on.

They walked around the corner of the house, then stopped short at the dismal view that confronted them. Flattened, scored earth surrounded the large empty space where the house had stood, visible even through the thick trees.

"You sure you're ready?" he asked.

She didn't speak, but gave a curt nod.

He took her small, gloved hand and helped her navigate through the thick snow banks. "Watch out, it's icy." Closer, he could see that the garage was still standing, charred by the flash of the explosion. There was hope for her truck, though the building was buried in sheets of ice and debris.

Alysia speeded up her steps despite his warning, striding around the perimeter of her destroyed dwelling and right to the garage, totally ignoring the huge black hole that had been her home until last night. He kept up, helping her the last few yards and letting go of her hand to push open the soot-covered main door of the garage. It was stuck fast and ice shards that had built up from the firemen's hoses rained down on him as he shoved his shoulder against the frozen door. It gave way with a loud, creaking groan. He pulled his gun and held it at the ready while checking out the interior.

When he was certain it was safe, he beckoned her in. "Is the truck locked?" he asked when she stepped through the doorway.

"No. And extra keys are in a small metal box attached to the frame over the back wheel well, driver's side."

"Good. It looks mostly undamaged. Might need a new paint job, though." He retrieved her keys and handed them to her.

"Thanks." He could only imagine what she was feeling, having seen her house blown to smithereens. No one could hide what they were made of, when in distress. But she held herself together with dignity, a quality he most admired, though he could see the strain of it in her pale complexion and tightened features.

He checked out the electric door, pushing the button to activate it, but it refused to budge. *Hmm.* He'd have to disconnect it from the drive chain. He went about the procedure, and soon had the door open for her. Then he stepped to the side to give her space to drive out.

She turned over the truck's motor and it roared to life. She drove out of the garage, only stopping briefly so he could jump in the passenger side.

"We can park it behind my parents' place, then take my vehicle into Hope to check in with your boss. All right?"

She nodded after a slight hesitation, her lips pressed together into a firm line. "Okay, but I take my truck to Vancouver and I refuse to argue about it." She stalled his immediate objections with a raised hand as she continued, "I'm not going to be without transportation. For Christ's sake, I just lost my home. I need my truck. I'm taking it and that's final."

He took a deep breath, willing some patience for her unreasonable behavior. The last thing he needed was her driving off somewhere unescorted in the sprawling megalopolis of Vancouver. It was then he noticed she looked different. He'd leave the arguing for later, when she was calmer. "I didn't realize you wore glasses."

"Yeah, made last night a bit challenging, though I can manage. Just a bit short-sighted."

"They look good on you." They did, giving her that sexy-business-woman vibe. She put the truck in gear and began driving the short distance to the street.

She shrugged. "Can't be bothered with contacts most of the time. Too much trouble."

She was acting distant, and he wanted to bring her back into the present. Being in the tight confines of the truck's cabin cocooned them in privacy, making him appreciate the fragrance of her freshly shampooed hair. The scent of berries filled his nostrils when she swung her head back and forth to check both ways on the street before proceeding.

"I called the office this morning when I left the room to have a talk with Walter. Explained the situation, gave the facts of the case."

"Ah, good." She winced. She finished driving the truck down his parents' driveway, both hands on the wheel, stepping on the brakes to park it beside the garage. He had a sudden realization. The house was now his, though he wasn't sure if he even wanted it. It held so many memories of growing up. Some good, some too painful to mention. *Time for that later.* Now he needed to be on his A game.

He disembarked while she rummaged in the back seat, dragging out a duffel bag. Taking it from her hands, he led the way into the kitchen through the back door, then laid the charcoal-colored bag on the table.

She took over, unzipping the top of the bag and checking out the gear. She pulled out jeans, a red T-shirt and a clear plastic bag obviously containing some underwear. He averted his eyes. "I'm going to take a few minutes to change my clothes before we go."

"Good idea. I don't think the outfit's quite you. You look like a cross between *Little House on the Prairie* and a diehard hockey fan."

She snorted. "Kind of the least of my worries. Not much point dressing up with the shitstorm my life has become. Besides, who'd notice anyway?"

He bit his bottom lip, dragging it between his teeth. Was this because he'd turned her down last night? Was she still upset about that? If only she knew how hard that had been for him. Just the memory of it made his cock begin to thicken and grow hard for the umpteenth time since they'd met.

"I'd notice."

"What?" She whirled around, already halfway out of the kitchen, clutching the small pile of clothes.

"I said I'd notice if you dressed up. Or didn't."

He'd surprised her. He could see it in the wide-open stare she gave before she looked away. "Well, I need to go shopping then. All my good clothes have gone up in smoke."

"After we get you settled in Vancouver, I'll take you shopping."

"Really?" A second glance of surprise gave him heart. It made him do something more, quite out of the norm for him.

"Sure, then dinner and a movie. Or maybe you'd prefer to go dancing?"

"You asking me on a date, Nick?" Sure, it was a crazy notion. But all they had was this moment. Who knew what further hell awaited them? An asshole willing to blow up a house was not an adversary to be taken lightly. Even with the entire TETRAD group on board, he knew better than to take any unnecessary chances. The problem was, did she?

"I think I just did."

"Maybe."

"Maybe what?"

"Maybe means maybe. I'll think about it."

"Don't think too long. Statute of limitations may apply in this case." Was he flirting, with all hell having broken loose? Somehow it worked, gave him a shift of focus, if just for a few seconds.

She laughed, albeit a bit shakily. It was the best sound he'd heard all morning. It warmed him to the core.

"I'll take my chances."

"You don't know what you're missing, beautiful. I do a mean two-step," he said, raising the ante.

She quirked her eyebrows, then vanished from sight. Had he come on too strong? Nah, he'd caught the glimmer of interest in her green eyes. And eyes never lied. That brought him full circle back to the case. Serious now, he shut down everything else and turned his attention to the matter at hand. Pulling out his phone, he sent a quick text to Jake Marshal, one of the founder members of the TETRAD group, to let him know he'd be bringing Alysia by the office later in the day. Jake and his wife Silk, Cole McClintock and his wife Gabby, Gabby's sister Celine, Quinn Malone and Nils, plus a few outlying operatives they could call in a pinch, made up the heart of an organization dedicated to helping those unable or unwilling to go to the cops. And he'd never needed them more.

Chapter Ten

Alysia locked the bathroom door, then leaned against it. She dragged a shaky breath into her lungs. Seeing her home destroyed, blown to smithereens, had cost more than anyone could know. As good as Nick was being about it all, it was of little help in absorbing the fact that her life as she'd known it, rebuilt from scratch, was gone. Totally blasted away to kingdom come. Or hell. Who knew for certain what waited? Down deep, a creeping suspicion slithered in that she must have done something to deserve it. *Sometime. Somewhere.*

No. No one deserved that. She had to believe it. She shook her head violently, chasing the bitter thoughts away, and struck back against the closed door with her fists, needing to pound something. *Anything.*

"Alysia, you okay?"

She froze. "Yeah, I'm good."

"Do you need something? Can you let me in?"

"No, I need to change yet." She swiped at the tears that had fallen unawares and were wetting her cheeks. "I'll be out shortly."

She felt him hesitate on the other side of the door, then heard footfalls as he moved away. She made herself act, take off her clothes and re-dress in her familiar things. It helped.

She fished an elastic band out from the pocket of her jeans and used both hands to pull all the wayward waves of hair to the crown of her head, anchoring them in place with the tie, fashioning a high ponytail.

"Better," she assured her reflection. She neatly folded the discarded clothes and picked up her cell phone just as it began to ring.

Unknown number.

She hesitated, mesmerized by the screen saver, thinking.

With trembling fingers, she pressed the Accept button on the lighted screen and held the phone to her ear. "Hello."

She glanced in the mirror again and straightened her bent spine, trying to look confident. Waiting for the person to say something, anything, she licked her dry lips. Creepy, raspy breathing echoed over the device. Frustration erupted after a few seconds of torture, intense anger following immediately on its heels.

"Who is this?"

"Now this is the point. You fancy me mad. Madmen know nothing. But you should have seen *me*. You should have seen how wisely I proceeded — with what caution — with what foresight — with what dissimulation I went to work!"

A short pause. She held on to the phone, clutching it against her ear, unable to stop listening, much as she wanted to.

"No one, I repeat, no one is safe around you." The words, so cold and robotic, and confusing at first, took her breath away, triggering a memory. Of a pre-teen obsessed with the writings of Edgar Allan Poe, certain they shared a common bond because of their last name. The quote was from *The Tell-Tale Heart*. She remembered it from having visited his bedroom. Once. As a child. Before she'd been warned to stay away. The walls had been lined with images and quotes of Poe. It was him. No doubt remained.

She threw the phone. Hard. It hit the edge of the marble counter with a loud *bang*, then smashed noisily onto the floor, bursting into pieces that scattered everywhere.

"Alysia, open up! Right now!" Nick's voice commanded from the hallway, his fist pounding on the door.

She held a palm pressed tightly over her breastbone, trying in vain to still the too-rapid beating of a heart about to explode. She unlocked the door and it crashed open, fueled by the passion of a man locked out.

"What happened?" His eyes flashed and the irises darkened to almost black when he grabbed her roughly around the shoulders, making her look him directly in the face. A glimpse of power stirred deep within the liquid depths of the open windows to his soul, a wild, thrumming current that promised more, much more than she'd ever experienced before. She had visions of being putty in his hands, his oh-so-capable hands. She shook her head violently to dispel the image, nearly overcome by the need to forget. But she wouldn't throw herself at him again, no matter how much she wanted it.

"I — I think it was him. On the phone. Just now."

She watched him glance away and down to the multiple pieces of debris littering the bathmat and titled floor.

"What did he say?" Back to staring at her, his eyes once more held her in his sway, boring into her with a frightening intensity. She was the first one to break contact. She decided at that precise moment what she had to do. For all their sakes.

"Nothing. Just did a creepy breathy number. Typical serial killer shit." She shrugged, chewing on the inside of her mouth.

He pulled her into a hug, his hands clasping her to his broad chest. "I'm sorry you had to go through that. Hell, all of it for that matter. The guy really is the monster you've described."

"It is what it is," she said against his chest, his warm breath tickling her cheek. The platitude came out in a flat tone of voice that sounded fake even to her. "You know, sometimes, I almost feel like —" She stopped herself just in time, pulling away from him to survey the mess on the floor. "You got a broom or a vacuum?"

"Ignore it. I'll deal with it later. You ready to go?" he asked.

"Yeah. Sure."

She pushed past him and exited the bathroom, Nick hot on her heels.

"I'll just leave a note for Walter. Let him know where we're going and that we'll be picking him up later." She watched him scribble a few lines on a pad of paper, then tear it off and attach it to the front of the refrigerator by a magnet with a happy face adorning it.

Soon as we get to Vancouver, I'm leaving. No fucking way I'm putting anyone else's life in danger.

Chapter Eleven

Poe held his head between his two hands. The urge to destroy, to silence the roaring in his head, was back, fueled by another fucking headache. *God damn it.* If she hadn't been out so late that night visiting her friend, he'd be pain-free now. This was all on her. He popped the plastic top off the prescription bottle with an impatient thumb and knocked a couple of the white pills into his mouth, chewing absently as he considered his options. He patted the top of Raven's head, the wolfdog's black tail thumping rhythmically on the wooden deck boards. He was grateful for his only friend, who was there for him no matter what, and hand-fed him some treats while he thought things through.

That damn woman had help now, if that guy he'd seen come to her rescue was going to take on her case. Decent enough help, too, if he trusted the reputation of the organization that called itself TETRAD, but not nearly as clever as he knew himself to be. *Go ahead, take her on, buddy.* He'd just become another pawn in Poe's long game. After all, his own intelligence was so far off the charts as to be one of a kind. No one could stop him. The very idea was ludicrous to the extreme.

He jerked back in his chair and put his boots up onto the rail of the recently constructed deck, watching a bald eagle soaring against the somber, gray skies. He took a deep, appreciative breath. The freshening in the wind suggested new snow before nightfall. *Hmm.* He needed to draw her out. And in a way that would benefit him the most, fulfill his deepest, darkest fantasies. So far, no one had caught on to his scheme — hiding the evidence in the mountainous terrain was easy, child's play. But it wasn't going to announce his presence to the world. Now was the time, he felt the righteousness of it in his bones. A crime that ensured a legend. They'd write reams of books about him and his clever, devilish mind. Something for others to admire for centuries to come.

Like Jack did.

He picked up the current true crime book on serial killers he was speedreading and reviewed the list of MOs of the worst of them from his handwritten notes on yellow stickies tucked into the pages. What would make the authorities' blood run the coldest? Something that hadn't been done before. That was a difficult assignment. It seemed the serial killer crowd could be inventive, or at least the few that were more intelligent and better organized.

He rubbed the scruff on his chin, considering. The draining of blood was a deviant act, along with satanic symbols or ciphers. Far worse than leaving a smiley face or can of beer at the scene like others had done in the past. But maybe a bit too vampire-esque, too trendy. And he certainly wasn't a messy butcher like Jack the Ripper or as hungry as Dahmer. An intelligent human being didn't let his emotions run amok, unless it became part of his deliberate game. Now H.H. Holmes, North America's first known serial killer, who reigned at the turn of the century, he sold body parts out of his inspired Murder Castle. A glimmer of how to modernize the scenario made him smile coldly. Beyond devious. Yes. *He plans. He schemes. He wins.*

He opened his favorite book—he needed just the perfect passage to leave as a calling card with the 'gifted' body. He thumbed through the dog-eared pages. Aw, there it was, from short story *The Black Cat*. No remorse seemed fitting. *'I soundly and tranquilly slept; aye, slept even with the burden of murder upon my soul!'*

A beeping sound on his belt that housed the off-grid GPS tracker alerted him to movement. He glanced at it, checking the reading. *Yes.* She was on the move.

Chapter Twelve

There was something Alysia wasn't telling him about the phone call. He was absolutely certain. She hadn't spoken a word since she'd gotten into his SUV for the drive to BC-STAR, keeping her head turned away from him the entire time, staring out at the landscape. Not that there wasn't a lot to see — the mountainous terrain held a lot of fascination for tourists and locals alike — but he'd bet ten to one odds she wasn't even aware of their location.

"Do you have any other unfinished business we need to take care of before we head into Vancouver?" he asked, turning the steering wheel of the vehicle and driving the SUV onto the lot that housed the trauma flight complex. He parked in front of the low-rise building bearing the familiar blue and white neon sign with its star signature logo over the doorway and turned off the motor.

"Sorry, what?" she asked, flicking a troubled, confused glance his way.

"What's the matter?"

"What? What could possibly be the matter?" she asked, attacking him with a gaze that flashed fire and brimstone. "Oh, maybe it's because my house has been blown up! Or a serial killer's on my tail!"

"I'm sorry."

She gave a deep sigh. "It's not your fault. And I'm the one who should be sorry. You've been nothing but kind to me. Well, except for turning down my invitation last night." She shot a second arrow, one with a wicked gleam attached.

"Hey, that's uncalled for. I had only your best interests in mind. You were vulnerable. I'm not going to take advantage of a woman who's in that state." He ran his hands through his hair in agitation, his eyes flashing with emotion.

"Well, don't worry, I'll not make that mistake again." And, with that, she yanked open the passenger-side door and jumped out.

Why was she being such a damn fool? Taunting Nick like that? She hadn't even known she was going to embarrass herself until it tripped right out of her freakin' mouth. Now she looked even more pathetic. God, she needed a drink. Too bad it wasn't even noon yet. Well, somewhere in the world it had to be cocktail hour. Right?

She burst through the front door at BC-STAR in her agitation, the noise making a couple of her cohorts look up in surprise. It was warm inside and she unzipped her parka.

"Alysia. How are you?" Jaqueline, a fellow trauma nurse, rushed over, enveloping her in a huge hug. Emily gave her a sympathetic look as well, continuing to pack supplies into a trauma bag. "We just heard about the fire and explosion. Are you doing okay?" She pulled back to look her in the face. The expression of kindness and concern in Jaqueline's blue eyes nearly did Alysia in. She had to look away, swallowing against the sudden constriction in her throat.

"I'm fine. No one was hurt, thank goodness. But I need to see Al. I have to take a few days off."

"Sure. He's at his desk. Is there anything I can do for you? See about your mail or anything?"

"No. I'm fine. But if you get the chance, could you check in on Kate? She's pretty isolated and lonely these days." Just thinking about her friend and having to be away from her hurt like hell. Of course, she'd call every day. But it just wouldn't be the same. That reminded her she had to get a cell phone ASAP.

"Of course. No problem. I'm sorry about your friend. I didn't get to work with her much at all, unfortunately, but I've heard such wonderful stories about her. You know—about her going beyond the call of duty to save a victim."

"Thanks." She swallowed against the rising grief. "She was one heroic nurse. I owe you. Anyone sleeping in the dorm at the moment?" she asked. "I need a few things."

"No. Go right in."

She hurried from the room before she embarrassed herself, and headed down the hallway. Passing the lunch room, she took a deep breath, enjoying the fragrance of fresh-brewed coffee. The dormitory for staff on duty was the next room over, the door closed tightly. She'd slept there more times than she could count, waiting for a call-out. Twelve-hour shifts with a five-minute essential response time to a call meant living at the complex while on duty. Sometimes, when shifts overlapped due to them being chronically short-staffed, she'd not made it home in days.

She gave a light rap on the door as a courtesy just in case. No answer. She twisted the doorknob and went into the brightly lit space. Normally homey, today it looked different. Stark and empty. Impersonal. Two sets of bunk beds lined one side of the room with the wall of beige lockers opposite, all numbered. The only bits of color were the patchwork quilts Kate had made covering each bed. She thought of the gorgeous log-cabin-style one her friend had made for her and tears prickled behind her eyelids. Burned to ashes. It had been her most prized possession after a happy photo of her parents on their honeymoon.

She blinked the tears away and hurried over to number five locker, where she punched in the combination to the keypad. She pried opened the narrow squeaky metal door that always wanted to stick, then pulled out a change of clothes and some personal grooming items in a clear plastic bag along with a six-inch blade secured in a leather strap. Tucking them under her arm, she exited past the two sets of bunkbeds and the sliding door that hid the small bathroom. She half-ran down the hallway to Al Hamilton's corner office, not giving herself time to worry about the upcoming conversation, which was bound to be difficult.

Al looked up from staring at his ever-present iPad at her quick knocks on the doorframe, his expression harried. The window blinds were open, giving a full view of the helicopter landing pad out back. The whirlybird, perched like a giant insect on the tarmac, gave the impression of always waiting for the word to leap up into the sky.

She'd rehearsed her short speech, but now it stuck in her chest. She hated to do this. It felt like she was letting the whole team down with her failure.

"Al—"

"Just the woman I wanted to see. Can you work a double on Thursday? Joyce needs time off. Her kid's got the flu."

Her heart sank. "Al, I'm sorry. I need time off as well."

His complexion whitened at her words, making her feel even worse, if that was possible. His gray-threaded hair standing on end from his trademark brush cut only added to the image of a put-upon boss. She understood, more than he knew.

"What! Now?" He shook his head as if trying to erase her words, his jowls moving back and forth from the vigor of the movement. She liked Al, which made this far worse. He asked a lot of his staff, but no more than he asked of himself.

"I apologize. But there's no help for it. If I didn't absolutely have to—"

"Kindly fill me in."

"I can't. It's complicated, and dangerous."

His dark eyes popped open at the suggestion of danger. She didn't want to say any more than she had to, but she needed to make sure he understood she would never lightly leave them in the lurch.

"I don't know if you've heard that my house was blown up last night?"

"No. God. I'm sorry to hear that." He was—she could read the flash of sympathy in his eyes. "I came in early and haven't had an opportunity to talk to anyone. It's this damn schedule keeping me tied to this desk." He gave the iPad a look of disgust. "I hate to ask this, but when do you think you'll be back?" he asked.

She hedged. "I don't know exactly. But the explosion at my house, it wasn't an accident."

His expression turned to horror at the idea, his eyes widening and boring into hers. "What do you mean, not an accident? What's going on?"

"I don't want you any more involved than you already are."

"Alysia Rossini, we've known each other for—what?—three years now. Surely you know that I just can't let you leave here without giving me some better explanation than that. Hell, I'd be worried every minute." His eyebrows came together into a tighter knit.

"No need. I have help from an agency that's going to protect me. A group out of Vancouver. TETRAD. That's where I'm headed now. And the less you know about the particulars, the better."

He drilled his fingernails on the wooden desk. A photo of his wife and daughter sat in a frame to his left and he caught her looking at it.

"How're Penny and Joy doing?" she asked.

A smile lit up his coarse features. "Great. Joy's just started kindergarten this past fall. Loves it! She's bright, just like her mother."

"Nice. I should go. Let you get back to work."

He let out a deep sigh he didn't bother to hide. "Please, stay in touch. Promise?"

"Okay," she agreed. "But I can't say how often. I think it might be a bit crazy getting to the bottom of things."

"No point in asking the bottom of what things?"

"No, but after this is all done, I promise to tell you."
That's if I'm still alive.

"I'm holding you to that." He got up awkwardly. He
wasn't a man who showed his affections, but she could
read it in his reddened eyes. They'd been through a lot
together. The calling—what they did on a daily basis—
had successes and monumental failures that could cut
a person to shreds. Everyone was aware of being one
death away from landing in perpetual hell on earth.

She took his outstretched hand, grateful for the
support. "Thanks," she murmured and quickly left his
office, her eyes tearing up. She swiped the evidence
away as she rushed down the hallway. She waved at
Jaqueline and Emily, hoping to make a quick departure.

"Hold on, Alysia. Something came for you a short
while ago," Jaqueline said. She hurried over and
handed her a small white envelope with her name in
block letters.

"Thanks. I gotta go. I'll be in touch." She avoided
Jaqueline's inquisitive look, taking the envelope from
her outstretched hand. She managed a small smile and
made a quick departure. She jumped back into the
truck and buckled up, keeping her eyes averted. She
tossed the plastic bag she was holding onto the floor at
her feet.

"How did you make out?"

"It sucked—okay? I'm letting them down big-time
with needing time off."

"Not your fault."

"Sure feels like it. If I hadn't brought that monster
back—"

"Don't go there," he said, a warning clear in his tone.
"Okay, I know life can suck and I don't have pearls of
wisdom about how best to get through it. But this is *not*

your fault. This is entirely about someone else's evil agenda. You did *nothing* to cause this. Hell, you've suffered as much or more than anyone."

Nothing to say to that. She turned and looked at him. At the concerned expression in his eyes, at his very presence that gave her something she couldn't define, except to say that he did give off a vibe, a glimmer of hope. Maybe it was because he hadn't run in horror at her predicament as any sane man would? He was putting himself in mortal danger just sitting next to her. No, it might not be her fault that a madman was stalking her, but it would be her fault if Nick got hurt because of her. She had to nip this. Today.

"I think we should head back now." She didn't look at him, just chewed at a non-existent thumbnail, the envelope neglected on her lap.

"I know what you're thinking."

"What? No one can know what another person thinks." She narrowed her eyes at him.

"I'm not letting you out of my sight. Just so long as you are aware of that."

"Not following," she said, giving him her best wide-eyed look.

"I see through your act, you know." He sat back, reclining against the leather bucket seat, looking comfortable, apparently not in any hurry to drive away. She swallowed her aggravation at being delayed. She was jumpy. Too jumpy. It was something she had to stay aware of if she was going to keep her wits intact.

"What act is that?" He intrigued her in spite of her reservations and knowing she should shut the whole thing down right now.

"You think this is all on you. It's not. You have help now whether you want it or not. And I know that you're hiding something from me. More happened in the bathroom during that phone call than you're admitting to. Just so you know, you can run, but you'll never hide from me again, baby."

Baby? She liked the moniker coming from his mouth almost as much as *beautiful*. But it was blatantly obvious she had nothing to say that would convince him of what she knew she must do. Silence looked like her only option. Nick started the motor and put the SUV into gear.

"We on the same page now?" he asked.

"Hmm." Noncommittal was safe. *Right?*

It was then she remembered the envelope. She turned it over and studied the markings. No return address. Her breath stilled. The innocent-looking white envelope turned vile, as though she was holding a snake that was coiled and ready to strike.

"What's that?" Nick asked, giving her a quick glance.

"Nothing. Just something from the office." She felt his eyes on her and she made herself relax. She'd open it later when she was alone. She thrust the offending envelope inside the plastic bag lying at her feet.

"Do you want to shop for anything in Hope before we leave?"

"No. I'm fine. I just want to get into Vancouver." *And lose myself in the crowds.* With two-point-four million souls in the greater Vancouver area, surely she could find someplace to hide? *Yeah. Who am I kidding?* Now that Poe had her in his sights, nothing would stop him. But, damn it, she couldn't just give up! Anger fueled the righteous spark growing larger in her brain. She had let this monster live. Now he wanted to kill her? *Where is the justice in that?*

Chapter Thirteen

Nick had never felt more uncertain about a woman in his life. Why was she locking him out? She'd been so responsive to him since the moment they'd met. Now she was different, like a whole play was going on in her head that he wasn't invited to. Was it just because he'd turned down her advances? She had to know that was the last thing he wanted to do. *God.* There was nothing more he'd like than to fuck her silly. Right here and now. Not like she wasn't the most exciting female he'd met in years—maybe ever. Was he wrong in his assumptions about her being too vulnerable? They'd both lost so much. He pushed back his own grief and kept his mind focused on the immobile, beautiful woman staring out of the window at the world. He was certain she wasn't seeing anything at all. Frustration made him slap the wheel with both hands.

"What?" she asked, giving him that innocent look that wasn't fooling him for a second.

"You know—last night—I thought we shared something special. Did you really not feel it too?"

"Sorry?" She seemed confused, biting at a thumbnail again.

"You are the most annoying woman, you know that?"

"What? Me! You've got to be kidding, right?" She turned her head and her eyes appeared filled with dancing fire. That was better. She was with him now, not drifting in a sea where he couldn't reach her.

"I'm not kidding. I want to help you. Hell, I got the whole office on your case right now, looking for Poe. Surely you can see your way to sharing any intel you have with me? Fair's fair, sweetheart."

Her eyes filled with tears, liquid pools of incrimination.

"Now what did I say?" His anger deflated in a heartbeat.

"My dad always called me that. Sweetheart." She took a deep breath, letting it out slowly. "Okay, Poe recited a verse from *The Tell-Tale Heart* on the phone."

"You mean the story that Edgar Allan Poe wrote?"

"Yeah. And he said no one is safe around me. He's right. You don't know him like I do. He's worse than a monster. In a category all his own. And he knows it." She shook her head, her eyes beyond sad.

Nick took his foot off the gas and headed the SUV into a rest area, where he parked and shut off the motor. The cloister of sway-backed spruce bent over from the headwinds that flew over the pass gave them some small measure of privacy. The fierce blasts of frigid air did their best to drain the life out of vegetation and wildlife alike. *People as well.* Even though it was freezing outside, he cracked a window to let in a bit of the fresh breeze to sharpen his mind.

"Why are we stopping?" she asked.

"We need to straighten a few things out. Okay?"

She didn't look at him, but crossed her arms over her chest and stared straight ahead.

"I don't know how I can be any clearer." He heard the anger in his voice and worked hard to soften his tone. "I'm concerned for your well-being, Alysia. When you pull away like you're doing, I feel you're hiding something. Something important that could make the difference between life and death. That might affect the outcome of my team. Do you understand what I mean? Just nod if you do."

"I've spent the last few years alone. No permanent boyfriend. Just men I've met on the road that I know will easily move on and not ask any personal questions. I never want anyone to be unsafe ever again because of me. Do you understand that?" She turned huge, questioning eyes toward him.

"I do." He reassured her. "But we can't let this bastard win. If you don't accept my help — TETRAD's help — that's what you will be doing, make no mistake. Letting him win. I can't let you do that. I *won't* let you do that."

The silence was deafening. He saw the struggle on her face, her lips pressed tightly together. It dragged out a few more precious seconds, making him sigh.

"Okay — okay. I think this is from him." She leaned over and fished something out of the clear-plastic bag at her feet. He took it from her outstretched fingers, a tingle making his arm muscle flex when their hands touched.

He inspected the small white envelope before breaking the seal on the back with a fingernail, slicing open the flap and withdrawing a business card. He read the words. Then recited them aloud. "*The boundaries which divide Life from Death are at best shadowy and vague. Who shall say where the one ends, and where the other begins?*" He gave her a glance. "It's signed Prince Raven. Do you know the quote? Or whom Raven refers to."

"I'm not sure about the quote. Maybe from *The Premature Burial*?" She shuddered in horror. "I'll check. But the name Raven's familiar. Poe had a puppy named Raven that went missing just weeks after he got him."

He got why she trembled. The idea of burial *before* death would strike fear into the staunchest heart.

She turned to him, giving him a twisted look of despair. "I don't have my phone. Could you check?"

He pulled out his cell and looked up the quote. "Yeah, you're right. Is this the first time he's left something for you at work?"

"Yeah. Until he broke into my house, I thought, you know, because I saved his pitiful life, he had called a truce. But now, this is out-and-out warfare."

"It's escalating. Makes me wonder." A sudden thought scared the hell out of him. "Maybe he's been doing this all along? I mean, why would he stop for so many years in between his first crimes and now? Yes, it happens, but it's rare. Generally, crimes of this nature escalate, become closer together."

"He'd never want to be thought common," she said in a bitter tone.

"A psychopath is controlled by his needs. He will slip up, make mistakes, no matter how clever he thinks he is. I'm going to have that angle investigated."

Nick noticed her shivering. He hit the electric button on the console to roll the window back up tight.

"You know the worst part," she said in a dull voice, staring out through the front windshield.

"No, what's that?" he asked when she didn't say anything more for a few seconds.

"I had a few things left from my family, nothing of monetary value, but very sentimental stuff. A few birthday cards, framed photographs, and a dog-eared copy of *The Paper Bag Princess* that my father would read to me every night at least twice." Her voice cracked. "And now they're all burned up."

"Hey, I'm sorry." He knew the words to be inadequate and he leaned over the center partition, placing his arm around her slender shoulders and pulling her closer. She laid her head against his chest. It made him dizzy. They sat like that for some time, watching snowflakes skitter across the pavement and occasionally swirl up in tiny gusting whirlwinds that would form a blizzard or tornado if they were on a larger scale. It was bleak and ice-cold outside. But right now, with Alysia snuggled in his arms, he didn't want the moment to end.

He pressed his lips to her silky hair drawn up in an elastic tie, breathing in the fragrance of cleanliness and a woman's musk and warmth. It stirred something inside him and he had to keep himself from moving and disturbing her.

"When this is all through, I'm holding you to that dance."

Her words broke his heart for her courage under extreme duress.

"Will it be my choice of location?" she asked, still snuggled under his chin.

"Of course."

"Then I want to strike one thing off my bucket list."

"What's that?"

"I want to go to Scotland and dance in a castle."

"You got it, beautiful."

He wanted to don armor for her, like his father had done for his mother. Whatever she needed, he would be there for her. A woman of such courage could never be abandoned. He wanted the time to find out if there could be more. If she would give him the chance, he could get them both through the fire. *Please, I need her to have faith in me.*

She pulled away, leaving him instantly bereft. "Okay, let's get this done."

Chapter Fourteen

Alysia felt strengthened by the short time in Nick's arms. Maybe she could let him in just a bit? Let him help? At least enough to see how this could work? If it didn't, it'd be easy enough to slip away. *Better I end things than allow this decent man to pay for saving my life. But please, please don't make me have to give him up so soon.*

She kept her expression calm as she made her decision, feeling heavy with the weight of it. She gave Nick a tight smile as he drove back out onto the highway, pointing the SUV toward home. In no time they were pulling back into the driveway of Nick's parents' house.

Nick shut off the motor. "Okay, I want this to go quickly. Stay close to me."

"You think he's hiding somewhere nearby?" The thought sent ice shards jabbing through her veins. She shivered, even though the parka was warm.

"I don't know. But I'm not taking any chances. Wait here."

He jumped out of the truck and drew his gun from its holster. He came around the side of the truck, opened the door for her and motioned for her to precede him down the path to the back door. "Watch your step."

She took a deep breath and stepped out of the truck. Did her back have a target on it right now, even as she walked at a fast clip toward the back door? She reached the house in a few strides and waited while Nick unlocked it in one swift motion.

"Get inside. I'm taking a quick look around."

"No, please, just stay with me." She couldn't see Poe shooting her down in broad daylight. Too risky. But she could never take a chance on being wrong with Nick's life also at stake. The floor beneath her feet tilted and swayed. Had she just made a terrible decision?

"I've got this. Go check if Walter's ready to leave."

She reached out to grab him, but his jacket slipped through her fingers. With a lump tightening in her throat, she watched him walk away. She had no choice but to close the storm door and head inside to collect his grandfather.

With a pulse roaring in her ears, she began calling for Walter. "Walter, are you here? We're getting ready to leave. Can you hear me? Walter!" She called louder when there was no answer to her first calls. She banged on a few closed doors. "Walter!"

"For Christ's sake, what's all the damn fuss about!" Nick's grandfather popped his head out from one of the rooms that lined the downstairs hallway, his expression beyond pissed, his black hair tousled. It was obvious he was naked behind the half-opened door. When he caught sight of her, he grimaced. "Sorry, got company. You just interrupted the last time Cheriè and I might be together. Come back in a half-hour."

She bit back a nervous laugh that threatened to spill over, not wanting to embarrass the old guy. He vanished back inside, closing the door with a loud bang. She understood all too well what was going on. Sex was one of the easiest ways to forget everything else. She shook her head as she tiptoed down the hall to the kitchen. *Might as well make more coffee.*

While it brewed, she spied the phone sitting on the counter. *Great. A landline.* In the mountains, most people had one due to times when cell service was intermittent. She picked it up and called her best friend. Kate answered after a few rings.

"Hello." The thin strains of her voice, hoarse from the cancer, made Alysia wince. She'd never get used to the devastating effects of the disease. People taken away from their loved ones one day at a time. Life didn't get much worse than that. *Except when it happens all at once,* she self-corrected. *No time to say goodbye.*

"Hey, girlfriend. How are you doing today?" She made her voice as cheery as possible. It was their daily ritual.

Kate cleared her throat, put a little more push into her voice. "Thinking of heading out and finding me some guy to fuck my brains out."

"Yeah, but you'd just leave him wanting more. He'd follow you home and become a huge pain in the butt. I'd advise taking care of it yourself. Or hire a gigolo. I'll even spring for the cost of some fancy dude to come and give you a lap dance."

"I might need a wig first."

"Nah, you got a sexy bald head. Nicely proportioned and all. While I got enough scars and bumps to make me look like the bride of Frankenstein." It was their daily ritual, and the blacker or the raunchier the humor, the better.

The back door opened and in came Nick. She let out a breath. He was in one piece.

"Say, I have to go to Vancouver for a few days. I just wanted to tell you that, but I'll call every day."

"Anything wrong?"

"No, nothing. Just need to take care of some things. I'll be back before you know it." She knew she'd wasn't fooling her. Kate was as astute as they came, but she was also compassionate and wouldn't pry.

"Okay. And don't forget to send that stripper guy right over. Hey, better make it two. I'm feeling particularly horny today and I've got lots of time slots open this afternoon."

Alysia closed her eyes. No way would she ever add to Kate's burden. Until this current situation was over, she'd need to hide everything from her dear friend.

"Tall, dark and handsome. Right?" She looked up at Nick standing by the freshly perked coffee, watched the kitchen light glint off his glorious hair. She had a new favorite hair color for men. A riot of golds, bronzes and browns that defied description.

He gave her a quizzical glance then poured two cups of coffee and set them down on the table, doctoring hers just the way she liked it—with a small dram of whiskey.

She cut off the call and joined him.

"Where's Walter? Is he ready to go?" he asked.

"Soon. Uh, he's a bit busy at the moment."

Nick raised his eyebrows. She met his eyes, giving him a blatant wink. And waited. The instantaneous look of realization was priceless. Talking to Kate had lightened her mood considerably. Kate gave more than

Alysia was able to provide for her, a situation she was acutely aware of. She owed her not only for that, but also for actually saving her life once in the field, shoving her right out of the way of a vehicle that had veered onto the side of the road. The out-of-control truck would have mowed her down as she knelt to retrieve supplies from her flight bag if not for her friend's quick actions.

"Trust Walter."

"Actually, I think he's the smart one here."

Nick's expression darkened. "If this is about—"

"Calm your horses. I just think your grandfather's kind of cool."

"Oh yeah? Wait until you've spent a few days in his company. You'll be singing a different tune, I guarantee it."

"Maybe. Time will tell, eh?" And at that moment she realized she was most likely going to get a few days to enjoy a family that was quickly proving to be the best distraction. Ever. Then a thought nudged out the good feeling and she had to ask. "Find anything outside that looked suspicious?"

"No. All was quiet—thank God." He downed the last of his coffee and washed and dried the cup before placing it back on the mug tree by the silver and black Bunn machine. She admired how tidy the house was kept. She liked things clean, everything having a place. *Where's my sanctuary now that my life has been blown to bits?* But not everything had been blown away. Just material things. She was still standing. In a room with a decent man. That was enough for this day.

"I'm going to round up a few things. If you want to borrow anything from my mother, just head upstairs. First door on the right's the master suite."

Not realizing she was going to, Alysia made for the stairs. Curiosity had got the better of her. She wanted to know more about the kind of people who had raised Nick.

Chapter Fifteen

"They had the real deal. A true love story," Nick said, leaning on the doorframe to his parents' bedroom. She whirled around, a stylized figurine of a man and a woman in her hands. The pretty, evocative silver and white porcelain piece showed them dancing, her white gown flowing out over his suit. Their expressions suggested that they were deeply in love, the piece highlighted by a large silver-colored heart formed behind the pair as though they stood under a trellis in an open-air garden. Nick had admired it often. It truly captured the love his parents had shared.

"It's beautiful."

A loud crash downstairs made them both jump. Wide-eyed, he gave her a curt directive. "Wait here!"

He raced down the stairs, drawing his gun. *What the fuck now?*

Walter stumbled half-naked down the hallway, holding his head. He caught sight of his grandson and gave a low growl. "Damn woman. Didn't take it well that I'm leaving and taking my...stuff with me. Robbed me blind and ran out. See if you can head her off."

Nick didn't move but stared at his grandfather.

"Well, aren't you going after her?"

"Quite frankly, I think she's earned it."

"Fuck's sake! That was five grams of high-quality —"

"Are you trying to be an albatross around my neck?"

"Why is every damn thing about you?"

"Everything okay?" Alysia asked. She stood in the hallway, her fists balled above her curvy hips. Nick forgot all about Walter.

"What do you think you're doing? Didn't I tell you to stay upstairs?"

She pursed her lips, narrowing her eyes. God, she was beautiful. His heart broke again for her plight. "No one, and I mean no one, tells me what to do, you — you turkey!"

Nick groaned. "Not you too. First my grandfather won't listen to reason, now you?" Why was he escalating things? He had no fucking clue. Maybe it was to see the fire in her eyes? No one wore defeat well. And he never wanted to see that look on Alysia even if he had to act like a bad guy to keep it from happening.

"I'll be in the kitchen when you and your grandfather get your shit together." She gave a dismissive wave of her hand and turned around, exiting the hallway.

"Got yourself a feisty one there, Nick-Nick. I'd put a ring on it, if I were you. Oh, and you owe me big money for the blow." And, with that parting shot, Walter strutted back to his bedroom. He missed seeing the finger directed his way by his pissed-off grandson.

Nick headed for the living room and the bar. He stood over the bottles of liquor, his hand hesitating over the golden-amber-hued decanter, a glass at the ready. *Shit.*

He had a long drive ahead of him. This wasn't the answer. No more drinking until this was all over. At least, not during the day.

He made an about-face and headed up the stairs to his bedroom to pack his few belongings. He didn't know how long until he'd be able to get back here. He'd have to call someone to check on things while he was gone, because he'd just decided he was keeping his parents' home, at least for now. Maybe one day he'd be prepared to live in it again. Have a family there.

Okay. It was time. He picked up the duffel bag and took one last nostalgic look around, glancing at the Superman bedspread his mother had made for him in his pre-teen years when he'd become enamored of the superhero. At the trophies he'd won in hockey, his favorite team sport. His mother had always kept his room at the ready even though he hadn't lived in the house for years and he'd mentioned often enough that she could turn it into a guest room or something else more useful. But she'd insisted. She'd wanted him to be able to come home again at a moment's notice. He should have told her how much he'd appreciated that. Tears filled his eyes and he blinked them away.

At least they had both known how much he loved them, because he'd shared that on his last visit during the summer out at the Green Lake. He had that, at least.

Setting his shoulders, he left his childhood room behind and went looking for Alysia. *Time to calm the lady down.*

Soon as he walked through the door into the kitchen, he picked up on her mood. Not good.

"Turkey?" he asked with raised eyebrows.

That stopped her for a moment, her mouth dropping slightly open with surprise. He glanced at her lips and saw the moment she caught him looking at her. A hot zing of passion passed between them that had nothing to do with the conversation—or maybe everything to do with it. "Nicer way of saying pain in my ass or asshole or shithead—"

He held up one hand in mock defeat. "Okay—okay, I get the idea."

"Do you? Because I don't think you do. I didn't survive this long without being proactive. I'm not going through my life being afraid of every little noise."

"Okay. You've made your point. But don't think you can change who I am, either. I have a strong drive to protect those I care about. Think of me as your new bodyguard."

He read the confusion in her expression. When she just stared at him, he was compelled to ask, "What?"

"You said you cared about me. You don't even know me."

"I know enough," he said in a gruff tone. "I know you're courageous, resilient, caring, morally solid—"

"If you're done with the ass-kissing, Nick-Nick, I'm ready to leave." Walter barged in, his gigantic leather suitcase banging against the floor and cupboards as he dragged the heavy load toward the back door.

Nick reached him in a couple of strides and took it away from him. "What have you got in here? Rocks?"

"Books. What else? Can't leave Zane Grey on his own."

"My grandfather loves a good western," he said over his shoulder to Alysia who stood and watched the proceedings. "You both wait here. I'll drive up closer to the door."

"What? Why do you need to do that? Too wussy to carry my load?"

"I love you too, Walter. Keep in mind that it's not too late to drop you off at the animal shelter, old man," Nick said. Alysia gave a weird snort, halfway between a laugh and a hiccup, then cleared her throat.

That shut Walter up.

"Don't think you'll be getting away with that!" Walter went red in the face. Nick knew the old man never liked the tables turned on him.

"Sorry, didn't mean that quite the way it came out." Nick made sure to keep his expression neutral. But he couldn't count the number of times his grandfather had stirred the pot and left him to pick up the pieces in the past years. "I'm just being careful about everyone's safety, so I expect you to pay attention when I tell you to do something."

Walter harrumphed and blessed him with the stink-eye, though thankfully remained silent.

"I'm taking my truck as well," Alysia said. She gave him a defiant look.

"No." He shook his head. "Absolutely not. It's not safe. We travel together."

He didn't give her time to answer, but strode outside to the SUV with the heavy case banging against his shins. He cursed and threw it into the back, slid in behind the steering wheel, placed the vehicle in four-wheel-drive and drove up close to the cement steps. Ignoring the deep ruts his tires were creating in the ice and snow, he jumped out and opened the back door of the house, gesturing for everyone to hurry up.

He didn't feel he could take a full breath until he had Alysia and Walter tucked safely inside the confines of the SUV and they were headed down the highway to Vancouver.

A few minutes later, Alysia leaned over the center console and whispered in his ear, "I think Walter's got some coyote blood in him."

The sheer unexpectedness of the comment made him burst into gales of laughter. She nabbed a chunk of his heart at that moment.

"What are you two lovebirds laughing your fool heads off about?" Walter grumbled, as if he somehow suspected he was the butt of a joke, his tone also suggesting he would prefer to be anywhere else in the world than where he was.

"What the hell, Walter! Can't you be decent for one hour?" Being called lovebirds just for sharing a joke was beyond the pale.

"I was decent until you came along. Decently enjoying my life, that is. Now I'm headed into who knows what with my grandson in tow. Not going to help with the ladies, I can assure you."

"Don't worry, I'm sure you'll see plenty of action at the local Legion Hall. My house is only a couple of blocks from one. And I have a whole suite on the first floor of my house reserved with your name on it. Has its own outside entrance and everything. You can come and go as you please."

"That so? Now you're talking." His grandfather rubbed his hands together, making a dry, rustling sound, his expression suggesting he was more than satisfied with that set-up.

"But if you bring home any illegal activities, I will be forced to change things up. Just so you know."

"A man of my age is allowed certain pursuits. Only fair after fighting for my country."

"Fine. Just so we're both on the same page. Are we?"

"Yeah, yeah, sure."

"Maybe Walter and I can spend time together?" Alysia said. "I play a mean game of checkers. Do you play, Walter?"

"Sure, make it poker and we've got a deal. Always ready to play with a pretty gal."

Conversation quieted as the snow began picking up, sleet hitting the windshield like popping corn. They were driving headfirst into a blizzard within half an hour. As soon as they got out of the mountains, things would clear on the descent into Vancouver. At least that was Nick's hope. He didn't want to take a chance on stopping. The sooner they got to his city fortress, the better. He kept an automatic lookout in the rear-view mirror for anyone shadowing them.

The business he was in, he'd taken the responsibility deadly seriously and built a bunker that appeared normal on the outside. Inside, he hadn't stinted on the safety features. No way he could lay his head down at night without knowing he'd done everything he could to keep those under his care from harm.

He ran his own witness protection program on the side. Being unmarried, he had the room and the inclination. And, at that moment, glancing over at his passenger sitting so tranquil beside him, he'd never felt more of an urge to protect anyone in his life. It was a living essence that surged inside him, growing stronger with each passing mile.

Chapter Sixteen

Alysia glanced over at Nick. He was so quiet, all his attention focused on the road. What he was thinking? It irked her to be totally dependent on him for a ride. As soon as they got to Vancouver, she was renting a vehicle. No way she was going to be hamstrung with waiting around if she had something she needed to do.

The snow had built up under the SUV's wipers, leaving gaps that wouldn't clear, obscuring visibility.

"I've got to stop and fix the wipers," Nick said. He drove the vehicle over to the roadside and climbed out, allowing gusts of freezing rain and snow to blow in.

"Shut the damn door already!" Walter complained from the rear seat.

Alysia sat up straighter. She didn't like having Nick out on the highway, vulnerable to the whims of traffic. He leaned over the hood of the SUV and used a gloved hand to swipe away the buildup of ice against the windshield. *Hurry up already.* She glanced over her shoulder and realized another vehicle was advancing to pass, only a few car lengths back. In a split-second fear rose and grabbed at her throat. The vehicle was too damn close! She watched in horror as the snow-covered van narrowly missed hitting Nick as he hugged the side of the SUV, the sounds of ice from the tires of the speeding vehicle pelting him and the fender.

"Fucking idiots!" Walter shouted from the back while shaking his fist at the receding taillights, his voice so loud it made her ears ring.

"That was too close," she said.

"Did you get the license number?"

"Covered in snow. All I got is a dark-colored late-model Dodge Caravan."

Nick finished his task and got in, shaking off a shower of ice crystals from his hair and clothing.

"You okay?" she asked. "That was close."

"Fucking drivers," Walter grumbled from the back seat.

Nick seemed unperturbed. "I'm fine. Road conditions are a bitch. The guy didn't have much room." He resumed driving. "Not far now."

Why was he making light of it? His eyes looked dead serious when he spared her a glance. "I need to rent a vehicle *and* get a new cell phone."

"I have an extra set of wheels you can borrow and a cell phone."

"Why on earth do you have two vehicles?"

"I take people in for TETRAD, those who need protection. That's why I have two suites other than my own. It's more of a bed and breakfast than a regular house. You'll have an entire floor to yourself."

"Wow." She really didn't know what to say to that, except 'thanks'. "That's very generous."

"Not generous enough. What about a sports car for me, Nick-Nick?" Walter grumbled from the back seat.

"The bus stop's not fifty feet from my front door."

"The bus? Fuck that! Excuse my language, young lady."

"Remember the last time you borrowed Mom's car? You damaged the front fender when you tried to run down that guy who stole your parking spot."

"That young punk had it coming. Taking a spot away from an old war veteran?"

Nick shook his head, his lips pressed tightly together. "Not going to happen on my watch. I'll hire someone to drive you around. Best I can do."

"Make it a pretty female and you got a deal."

"Almost home," Nick said, giving her a quick glance.

Home. She liked the sound of that. With his hair still damp from the snow and his cheeks flushed from the cold, he looked virile. *Good.* Her fingers itched to push back a lock of bright hair that had fallen over his forehead. If it wasn't for Nick and Walter, she wasn't sure how she'd be doing. Even the bickering helped, kept her from focusing on anything else for healing moments of time.

Ten minutes later, Nick turned the SUV onto a side street near Grandville market. "I'm just over there." He pointed at a huge white-framed house with black trim and red shutters. She liked the look of his home. It did indeed look like a prosperous bed and breakfast. For some reason she had expected all chrome and modern edges. His home was an anomaly in an area that featured mostly modern architecture.

He pulled down the overhead visor and pushed the button that activated the electronic eye on the double garage door. He drove the wet vehicle inside the space attached to the house and turned off the motor. The massive door came down behind them, sealing them in. A second vehicle, a black Mercedes, was parked in the twin stall.

"Nice place," she said, giving him an appreciative smile.

"I wanted something inviting. Nothing cold and ultra-modern. I think it helps anyone who needs a safe haven. And it was big enough to allow me to build in some safety features. Only thing it doesn't have — a moat. But it's got everything else, including a safe room on each floor. Be careful when you get out — the vehicle's covered with slush and salt. And that car next to us, the keys are always in the ignition in case of emergency, just so you're aware."

"Good to know, thanks." Alysia opened the door and jumped down to the cement floor of the garage, stretching her cramped legs.

The three of them hurried through the connecting door and Nick gave them a quick tour. They dropped Walter and his books off on the ground level, then took the elevator to the third floor.

"You've got the whole floor to yourself. I'm down one. Being sandwiched in the middle allows me quicker response time if anything happens."

"This is really nice," she said, giving the three rooms a quick perusal. A large bedroom, sitting room and bath. "You could make a fortune renting it out to tourists."

He shrugged. "Not my style." He went over to a sideboard and pulled open a drawer. "Keys for the house are in here. The safe room is located through that door." He strode over and pointed out how it worked. "As soon as you enter and close the door, press this red button. The door automatically locks. Then an alarm goes off here and at the security company downtown. They call the police immediately."

She peeked inside. Heavy steel walls with a few amenities. Water, a chemical toilet and packages of non-perishable food. A comfortable cot with a pillow and blankets neatly stacked on top. "You went to a lot of trouble."

"I want you to feel safe. And the whole building has a built-in sprinkler system."

He stood closer. He had the look of a guardian, a warrior. Goosebumps erupted on the surface of her skin.

"Thanks." In truth, even though it was intellectually a safe bet, a part of her felt the shadow of unease that lay over her life and loomed at the darkest recesses of her mind, always ready to squeeze her in its deadly grip and snuff the life from her. While Poe was free, she never would be.

"I know you don't totally believe it, but I will find him. And, until I do, you'll remain at my side. Can you do that? Promise to keep yourself safe—for me?"

She pressed her lips together, unable to answer. *Why did he have to ask that?* She could no more promise him to always do what he wanted than to fly him to the moon. She hadn't made it this far by doing what others wanted. She'd made it with grit and determination not to let evil win. And yet she knew he had her best interests at heart.

The war within her raged. The times when she should have felt the safest were when she was most afraid. A sense that if she let her guard down for one second, the worst could happen. *Would happen.*

She felt his hands on her. Then she was in his arms. He held her tight, his heart beneath her cheek, the steady pumping beat of it echoing in her head. She breathed in his essence and her inner core squeezed with need and desire.

"I know you're afraid. You have every right to be. And I know that it's just words you've been hearing so far," he murmured against her hair. "But when the day comes that I can show you, prove to you that I will do everything in my power to keep you alive and, well, you just have to believe it — believe me — that I will die trying."

"Oh lord," she whispered, her knees weakening. A feeling of such need shuddered through her entire frame that she lost all sense of perspective. "Please, make me feel something. Something good. Take me. Now."

His entire body stilled. She felt the instant thickening of his cock, his groin pressed tight up against her lower stomach. Scorching heat erupted deep inside her, caught fire. *Yes.* She rubbed against him, a low moan escaping her lips. "Yes, please, fuck me. Fuck me hard. Talk dirty to me." She loved dirty words, had always insisted on them in the past. *Anything to forget.*

He fisted her hair and tugged out the elastic band holding her ponytail to run his hands through the silky lengths of it. He eased her closer, tangling his fingers in the long curls, and took her mouth. *Passion.* The heat of his lips, his tongue, his hands caressing her skin.

One hand slipped down between her legs while she reached for his cock, rubbing it through the thick material of his jeans. It was hard and she wanted him buried deep inside her. His naked body grinding into her, making her come over and over until neither knew where one ended and the other began.

Nick moaned, his voice low and throaty. "You don't know what you're asking. I want you so badly, but I would be taking advantage. We should wait. We barely know each other."

"I know exactly what I'm asking and I'm not drunk. I'm consenting right here and now. I want you inside me. I want you to fuck me like there's no tomorrow. Is that too much to ask?"

"No — yes, maybe. I want to taste you, kiss you, have you in every way." He crushed her against him, his hot breath and body already a part of her. *So good.*

"Then take me. All of me. Now, before I explode."

She unbuckled his belt, pulled down his zipper, grasped his thick cock and caressed the full length of it. She had broken down his last defense. He was a man, his body's actions primordial. He would do as she asked. It was built into his DNA, giving her control at this moment. *Nothing sexier than that.*

"You want me. Have me, Nick. Make use of that fine, big cock of yours. Sink it into my hot, wet pussy. I know what it wants — just let it happen. Feel it. Let our bodies take over. Take us to the moon and back." The words swept from deep inside her, a place of hidden magic.

His last defense down, he shucked off all his clothes, revealing the firm flesh underneath to her hungry gaze. She did the same and removed her glasses as well, her eyes locked with his, standing naked before him in a matter of seconds. The connection between them was undeniable. The electricity sparked, hot and real.

"You are so beautiful. I want this moment to last. Let me show you how. I want to make love to you, not just fuck you." His voice held such reverence that she was struck dumb for a few seconds.

He reached out one hand and trailed his fingers down her body with such a gentle, loving touch that it brought instant tears to her eyes. No one had ever looked at her like that. Treated her like she was a fragile flower. It gave her pause and made her want to open herself in a new way.

She realized then that they weren't going to have the usual quick, necessary fuck, but something more.

Something she'd never experienced before. There had always been an essential quality to the act that she had sensed was missing. Never wanting someone to get too close to her had kept her from feeling much beyond the obvious. To take a chance on her baggage harming anyone else had always felt wrong.

Confined her.

Defined her.

Nick tweaked the tip of one of her breasts, bringing her back into the moment. The intimate caresses sent signals of lust and want and need and caring to her brain. A strange mix of emotions filled her, made her feel new again.

As if it was her first time.

Maybe it is…

She grasped the back of his neck and pulled his head down close to her chest, wanting to feel his lips on her. He obliged and began kissing her breasts, sucking gently at the nipples, a touch that turned her on more than all the extreme things she had tried before.

"Make love to me, Nick," she said, her words different, her tone different, her hands on his body different. *All different.* Not fired by near violence, half-drunk, but instead fueled with the strength of caring.

"Ah, beautiful, now you're talking my language."

She closed her eyes.

He picked her up in his strong arms and bore her to the bed. He pulled back the covers and laid her down then kissed her on the lips, his tongue seeking, tasting and nibbling at the tender flesh of her neck. She shivered. It was past time for this. She'd wanted him since she'd run into his arms, when he'd made her feel safe for the first time in a decade.

But he made her wait longer, teasing her, making her want him all the more. She opened her eyes and watched as he made love to her flesh, worked his way to her breasts and gave each his full attention.

She grew wetter. An ache filled her and made her mangle the sheets, twisting them in her hands. She forced herself to wait now. To let him do it his way as he worshiped her skin, finally making his way to the apex of her thighs. He spread her legs apart and kissed her most sensitive spot.

She grasped his hair and held on tightly, driven near insane by the onslaught of incredible sensations his fingers and lips were drawing from her. Her breathing became harsh. Ragged.

"Oh, don't stop. It feels *so* good," she whispered, opening herself to him. She succumbed to the lust building inside her, wave after wave of pleasure coursing through her before she hit her ultimate climax. It loosened her mind and body from everything else. Allowed her to drift free in time and space.

He stopped to tear open a condom and pull it on while she waited for him to come back to her, still shuddering with the first release of tension. She needed more, so much more. She needed *him*.

He climbed on top of her, spread her thighs farther and thrust his hard cock into her, sliding it all the way home. She gasped, stretching to accommodate him. Aided by her readiness, he thrust in and out, his powerful thighs guiding him into her with each shove of his groin, each push of his glutes, his balls hot and heavy between her thighs, slapping against her and adding so much power to him. To the amazing moment.

"Yes, *oh yes*." She encouraged him, her body coiling and preparing for another orgasm, stronger, more intense than the first one. Sweat rolled off them as they pushed themselves to the limit. Flying free once more, each second lifted her higher and higher. His body shuddered as he gave of himself, filling her with the heat of his climax.

He cradled her with one arm and pulled up the covers around them with the other hand. Cocooned, they lay face to face, staring into each other's eyes. She saw herself reflected in the liquid pools of light. She never gave the men anything back after mutual needs were satisfied, but this time she raised a hand to his face and traced the outline of his profile. A strange feeling filled her. *Tenderness and awe.* She'd never been to that place before. Sex had become an escape action without any depth of feeling, always leaving her with the thought to just keep moving. This was new. She didn't know how she felt about it yet. It was enough just to feel.

She ran a finger over his lips. He playfully nipped at it, sucking the digit into his warm mouth. She smiled, then cuddled closer to him, listening to the strong beat of his heart. *Thumpa. Thumpa. Thumpa.*

Chapter Seventeen

Nick slipped his arm out from under Alysia's neck, eased her back onto the pillow and snugged the blankets around her sleeping form. He leaned down and kissed her forehead, lingering for a few seconds. She had never looked more peaceful in the short time he'd known her.

He left the room, spurred on by all he had on his plate at the moment. But his number-one impulse was making damn well sure nothing happened to the woman in his bed, even if he had to tie her to it to keep her from running into danger. They were connected now. The game had forever changed for him. If he'd been driven to keep her safe before, now it was an obsession.

He was on his phone when she hurried into the kitchen. He sat at the table on the second floor of the building, boots outstretched as he leaned back on one of the sturdy wooden chairs. It was one of his favorite spots overlooking his Zen garden, one that always allowed him to think more clearly. Alysia looked good, obviously freshened up by a shower and wearing the clean clothes she'd picked up from BC-STAR. She gave him an exasperated look as he ended the call. "Why didn't you wake me?"

"I thought you could use the rest. Are you hungry?"

Loud gurgling answered his question as she joined him, sitting down across from him at the kitchen table. He watched her glance out of the window. There was so much he wanted to say, but he held it in. She was back to being the beautiful, mysterious Alysia. Unflappable. *Good.* She'd need all her wits and strength until they had seen this mess through to its logical end—Poe captured or dead. "I've ordered pizza. It should be here shortly."

"I love your garden. Pizza sounds good. Then we're to meet with TETRAD?"

He nodded. "Cole Marshal and Quinn Malone. Should be here within the hour."

"Here?" Her light green eyes zeroed in on his with laser focus.

"I'd rather not expose you to the outside world until we have a location on Poe."

"Phhht. I'm not sitting around here all day." Her peaceful expression vanished.

He didn't say anything for a moment, reminding himself to be patient. With strength of character came conflict, and their coupling had made them both stronger. *Good.* He wanted his woman to be strong. Just not to take chances. "Here's the deal. You need something, anything happens while you're out, I'll be your extra pair of eyes and ears. Together we make a united front. And we can watch each other's back."

She chewed on her bottom lip, staring out of the window. He reached over and kissed her. Quite thoroughly. He pulled back and tucked a stray curl behind her ear.

"You think kissing will work? Keep me compliant?" she asked. But he caught the flash of a twinkle in her eyes before she shut it down.

"Maybe. Either way I win. I get to kiss those sweet lips of yours."

"Flattery won't work."

"You sure about that?"

The doorbell rang.

"I'll get it. Wait here."

She rolled her eyes and he had to keep himself from swearing. She was not going to make it easy for him. That was clear.

Nick strode down the hall to the front door and checked through the peephole, recognizing the pizza delivery guy, Marcus. Even so, he kept alert as he opened the door and paid him for the pies with cash, plus a generous tip. The smart way to go when one wanted all transactions to be untraceable.

He watched Marcus walk away and get into his compact car. He looked up and down the street, making sure the man hadn't been followed. The delicious fragrance of the pizza drifted upward as he triple-locked the reinforced door. The spicy aroma made his own stomach rumble. It had been hours since breakfast.

He carried the pizzas to the kitchen and set them on the table. He went to the cupboard and got two plates while Alysia opened the lid of the first red and white box.

"What?" he asked, catching her odd expression. She pulled out a note taped to the inside lid of the box.

She read it. Handed it to him. Didn't say a word.

"'*TETRAD is not the answer. Only you can save the others.*' What the fuck?"

"What others? What do you think he means? What's going on, Nick?"

The horrified expression in her eyes made him wince with pain. How the fuck had this happened? How had Poe managed the near impossible? He'd been careful, had more than one place he ordered food from in random rotation. There was nothing he hated worse than being fucked with, and seeing the worry in Alysia's eyes made him so furious he wanted to strangle Poe with his bare hands. *How dare he, the fuckin' scumbag.* He took a deep breath, tamping down the roiling anger. He needed to direct the anger to find this fucker. *Think, damn it.*

Okay. The guy had to have followed them here even though there had been no sign of him other than the possible near-miss on the highway, but he'd made absolutely certain that vehicle had not followed them into Vancouver. Then he must have been watching somewhere nearby and stopped the pizza guy, bribing him, which meant he already knew where he lived from before.

Of course, he had visited his parents' home enough that the guy must have noticed, put a check on him, meaning he had been watching Alysia for some time. Poe could have known all about him and TETRAD *before* the recent series of incidents had begun. There was no other way this could have happened. *Damn it all to hell.* This put a new complexion on it. Things were escalating. The bastard's MO had changed, leaving a direct threat rather than a mysterious quote. He swallowed back the bile that burned his throat. That fucker was going down.

Okay. First, he needed to talk with Marcus. Find out what he knew. Could Poe even be on surveillance camera? CCTV lined his property, filmed every square inch. His hunger had vanished. He lunged to his feet. "Wait here. I won't be long."

"No. I'm going with you. I'm safer with you, right?" She had him and he could tell by her expression she knew it.

"Fine. Grab your coat."

He backed out of the garage, keeping a sharp eye out. Drove the short distance to Mama & Papa's Pizza. He parked and got out, Alysia right behind him. There was no point in telling her to wait, she'd defy him anyway. And now they truly were in this thing together, the outcome mattering as much to him as if his own life was at stake. Because it was, at least the part that mattered. With his parents gone, Alysia and saving her had become his lifeline.

He pushed through the door of the pizzeria, holding it open just long enough to allow her to slip in first. He wanted her where he could see her at all times. The delicious fragrance of garlic, tomatoes, and cheese grilling at high heat reminding him he hadn't eaten. Never mind, it just made him sharper.

He grabbed Alysia's hand to keep her by his side. From now on they would be conjoined twins, no matter the ruckus it caused him.

"Is Marcus here?" he asked the waitress at the counter who stood waiting for their order.

"He's out on a delivery. He'll be back soon. You a friend or relative?" she asked, chewing on the end of a pencil and giving him a look of inquiry. She wore the trademark red and black striped apron with the logo for Mama & Papa's Pizza stenciled on the front in white embroidery.

"We'll wait. I'm a customer."

"Something wrong with your pizza?" she asked.

"No, it's fine." He turned away and kept watching for activity on the street, not wanting to be ambushed. "I'll handle the interview," he whispered to Alysia.

Noise sounded in the back of the takeout-only restaurant a few tense moments later and the waitress left to check on it. He heard a short conversation.

Marcus popped his head in, looking worried. He came forward reluctantly, dragging his heels. He looked to Alysia then back at him.

"You wanted to see me?" he asked, crossing his skinny arms over his black T-shirt, which displayed the same logo as the waitress's did.

"Did someone stop you on the street today and ask you to put something into my pizza?" he asked bluntly. He had no time or patience for fools today.

"No. Maybe. Why?" he hedged. The waitress had come back and was quite interested in proceedings, watching them without shame.

"The guy left a threatening note."

"What? He said it was supposed to be funny. That you'd be laughing at it. Damn, I'm sorry, mister. I had no idea. Guy seemed really nice. Said he was a neighbor and that the two of you played pranks all the time. You know, like those TV shows where someone is always being hit on."

"Did he pay you?"

"Ah, yeah, quite generously. Do I get to keep it?"

Nick shrugged. "Fine. Just describe him to me, explain where you met him, and we'll call it even."

"I had just turned onto your street when he flagged me down. I think he got out of a dark-colored van. He came right up to my window. He asked who I was delivering the pizza to? If it was the fancy house with the Victorian motif? I said yeah, and he told me about all the pranks you guys play. Said if I wanted to make an easy fifty bucks, all he wanted was to tape a funny message inside the box. It sounded innocent enough." Marcus swallowed, his Adam's apple moving up and down.

"What did he look like? What was he wearing?"

"Tall guy with big build, like he worked out with weights a lot. He wore dark jeans and a black bomber-style jacket. Black hoodie pulled up over his head. Dark hair. He seemed nice enough. I'm real sorry about this. I had no idea. Here, take the money." The kid reached into his jeans and pulled out some crumbled bills.

"No, you keep it. The description helps. Would you recognize him again? Did you happen to notice a scar on his forehead? Or the color of his eyes?"

"Sorry, didn't look that close, but I'd probably recognize him. He was wearing sunglasses so I didn't see his eyes. He going to be in a lineup or something?" Marcus perked up.

"No, but I may come by with a photo later. You up for that?"

"No problem. Glad to help." The young man looked relieved, obviously wanting to make up for his critical error in judgment.

Nick assisted Alysia from the joint and they quickly got back into his SUV.

"What next?" she asked as she buckled herself in.

"Check surveillance footage. See if we can spot the guy. Did the description fit Poe at all?"

"He didn't work out with weights, or at least was still thin last time I saw him—you know, when he had the accident—so I can't be sure."

"Then I dearly hope we have him on camera."

Chapter Eighteen

Alysia chewed on a fingernail, her heart fluttering uncomfortably. She checked out every face they passed on the street. Was he watching them right now? Hidden nearby? She shouldn't have come. She'd placed Nick in danger — a man who had just lost his parents. She'd put her own needs first, and it wasn't right.

But what could she do? Leave the country? Live in exile? No. She couldn't do that. *Sweetheart, follow your heart.* She blinked back a rush of tears as her father's voice filled her head. What was that supposed to mean? Her heart wanted to be with Nick. He gave her so much, made her feel so much better about herself. It was so new, so precious, to feel that way.

She glanced over at him. He drove competently, like he did everything she'd watched him do so far. She ached to hold him again. To relive the freedom they'd experienced just a few short hours ago.

"How are you doing, Nick?" she asked.

"I'm good."

"Yeah, you are that." He gave her a quizzical look. "Good, I mean. And you're also good at doing things."

He blinked. "So are you."

"Why did I save that fucker's life?" That was what was eating at her. This wouldn't be happening otherwise.

"We've been through this already." Nick let out a deep sigh. "I told you not to focus on it. You did the right thing. No one can take that away from you. Save your energy for what's coming, beautiful."

"Why are you being so good to me?"

"Why? You need to ask that?" He seemed genuinely surprised, making her ashamed to be bothering him with so much going on. She was so much stronger than this. She'd let the note in the pizza box throw her for more of a loop than she'd realized. *Get it together.*

"Sorry. My brain's in a funk."

"Don't apologize. Good. My guys are here."

She turned from staring at him to observe a couple of large vehicles parked on the street in front of his house. One black SUV with dark-tinted glass, barely within legal limits, and one silver Hummer looking loaded for bear.

Great. Reinforcements. Nick needed his friends and co-workers around him now more than ever. That reminded her to give Kate a call later, make sure she had everything she needed.

Okay, clear your mind.

She took a few cleansing breaths while Nick parked the vehicle in the garage. She followed him into the house and up to the kitchen on the second floor where two men appraised them as they walked in together.

"Hey, Wheeler Dealer," one of the men said with a half-grin.

She turned and looked at Nick. "Wheeler Dealer?"

"Old nickname from college."

"Yeah, because you knew how to strike an excellent bargain on anything we needed. You wanted it, this guy could get it for you, no matter what it was. Hell of a gift. He understands the human psyche like no one else I've had the privilege to meet. It's come in handy for all of us at TETRAD many times."

Nick made a quick introduction while she checked out the two men at the table, looking at each in turn. "Alysia Rossini, I'd like you to meet two of the founding members of the TETRAD group. Jake Marshal — former military — and Quinn Malone — former FBI."

They were big, strong-looking men. Quinn had a short military haircut while Jake, the one who had called Nick the Wheeler Dealer, had nearly black hair a bit longer on top, enhanced by a full beard. Both wore an air of quiet confidence about them. Easily likeable. She glanced at the pizza box open on the table, noting that a few slices were gone. The note was re-folded and set off to the side.

"We made ourselves comfortable. Seemed a shame to just let the pizza go to waste," Jake said. "Besides, my wife never lets me eat enough of this stuff even though I've explained it should take up one entire section of *Canada's Food Guide*."

She glanced over at Nick, who caught her look of inquiry. "His wife, Silk. They have a baby boy. Cole Quinton Jake O'Connor-Marshall. Quite a moniker for a little baby."

"Not such a baby anymore. Cole's fifteen months, walking all over the place, into everything and running his parents bloody ragged." The big man dressed all in black shook his head with a big smile on his face. "Where he gets the energy from, I'll never know." His sleeves were rolled up, revealing stylized tribal tattoos on his forearms.

"I'll make some coffee," Nick said, gesturing for her to sit.

"I'd rather have some of that low-alcohol beer if you have it?" Jake asked. Quinn gave a grin of approval.

Nick pulled four cans of lager from the fridge and placed them on the table in front of them.

"We ran into Walter when we arrived." Quinn popped the pull tab off his beer and took a swig. "Told me to tell you he was headed to the Legion. Not to wait up. He expected to have female company later."

Nick snorted. "Figures. Walter's incorrigible."

"You know, with this psychopath roaming loose, you might want to keep Walter on a shorter leash. The guy could use him as leverage."

"Shit! I never thought of that." Nick's face instantly darkened with worry.

Alysia knew it was his concern over her situation that had interfered with his thinking of that outcome for Walter. The weight of it made her feel nauseated.

"I'll have someone keep an eye on him," Quinn said, sending a quick text on his phone.

"Thanks. I owe you one," Nick said.

"One?" Quinn said with a laugh before continuing in a far more serious tone. "Heck, man, we all owe each other our lives. No biggie."

Alysia appreciated the affection that rolled between the three men, thinking how it mirrored her own experience in the trauma unit of BC-STAR. Life-and-death situations changed a person's perspective. Those involved tried to make every moment count for something.

"We saw the note. The guy's a sick fuck all right. It's going to be a real pleasure taking him down," Quinn said, running a hand over his short salt-and-pepper hair. He added a wicked grin.

Three warriors. All on her side. Her definition of the perfect storm.

"Nils has worked round the clock sleuthing out every last bit of data on Poe," Jake said, moving his chair closer and giving his beard a rub with the palm of his hand.

"Nils?" she asked.

"Only the best tech guy on the planet," Quinn explained.

"The guy's mostly been off-grid for the past year. Been careful, though not careful enough. He's surfaced a couple of times. Once at a café right here in Vancouver, not far from this address, and once at a downtown public library. Both times Nils caught him on camera. He has an electronic library card and at the café he brought a computer with him," Jake said.

"Which café?" Nick asked.

"Timmy's—near the mall entrance on McGilvery. He ordered an extra-large double-double and a pastry," Jake said.

"Which library?" she asked.

"Centennial Library."

"I've spent a lot of time there," she said with a shudder, thinking of Poe walking those hallowed halls. "When I was in college, taking my nurse's training."

"Nick said you work for BC-STAR?" Quinn inquired.

"Yeah, the last few years. Been good. Until now, that is."

Jake patted her hand lying on the table top. "We'll make it good as new."

She smiled. Something eased in her chest. She was not alone anymore.

"I think there may be other victims," Nick said. "His note alludes to them. And someone like that—I find it hard to believe he's been sitting on his ass all these years. He's been busy perfecting his scenario. He fits the profile of an organized killer with control fantasies and they're compelled to act them out. Hit the data harder, guys. Has he been seen with anyone? Do the police think there's a serial killer on the loose in Vancouver? Anyone been abducted on the day he was there near the library? Or the café?"

"Sounds good," Quinn agreed. "How about what happened today? You want Nils to check the street surveillance?"

"No, I'm on that."

"Now that he knows you're in Vancouver, the chances of drawing him out are better," Jake said.

Quinn gave a nod. "Yes, I agree. Nils hasn't located his home base yet, but he's working on it, checking all the land titles. The guy has also chatted in the past on a survivalist chat forum—called himself *MountMan1*. Nils figures it's close to Hope, up a mountainside. He'd been careful to bounce his signature through a number of IP addresses, but Nils is working on triangulating the signal if he uses the site again. Get that, we get him."

"But now he's in Vancouver he won't be online for the forum, right? And even if he is, the address will be incorrect." Alysia saw the flaw in the plan. "I think the land titles is the best option. He'd have to use a name for that—unless he's squatting."

"Yes, you're right, we have to wait on that until he's back home again. At some point he will be. It's just a matter of time until we nab him. The bastard will slip up. Hell, he already has by using the internet at all."

"That's true," she said, chewing on a fingernail. "He always thought he was smarter than everyone else. Maybe if he gets too confident..." She left the idea hanging in the air.

"Okay, that's about all we got at the moment. We'll keep in touch," Jake said.

"Send me the photos Nils got of Poe at the two locations," Nick said. "Marcus at the pizza shop described the guy who bribed him to bring in that damn note and I want to check it out."

"Will do. Catch you later. Thanks for the pizza and beer, buddy. Nice to meet you, Alysia," Jake said.

Quinn echoed the sentiment.

The two men took their leave. Alysia waited at the table, listening to the indistinct voices, drumming her fingers on the top. The thought that maybe right this moment Poe was stalking another victim sickened her soul.

Nick came back into the room. "I'm going to check if we caught him on camera."

"I'll join you." She needed something to do. Something to take her mind off her deepest worry. That someone might die in her place. Could she live with that? She had no idea. Some things were impossible to imagine until they were faced.

Chapter Nineteen

Nick led the way into his study and booted up his computer system. He had numerous cameras about his property, connected to a series of screens shared over three monitors and all set up courtesy of Nils. At the moment they showed only a man out walking his dog. Alysia sat beside him. He breathed in her fragrance, like sunshine and roses, taking it deep into his lungs. Hmm, he'd better watch out or he'd not be able to keep his mind off what he would rather be doing. He made himself focus on the screens, hard as it was when all he wanted to do was take her to bed. Again. And again. *Later*, he promised himself. After he had made her safe.

"You want to watch the screen that shows the sidewalk to the front door? I'll check out the ones that lead down the street," he said.

"Sure."

Nick watched her cross her long legs and rub the back of her slender neck with one small but very capable hand. He fought the urge to kiss the soft stretch of skin left exposed by the ponytail she'd drawn her hair into.

They both stared intently at their assigned screens, the only sounds the antique mantel clock tick-ticking the seconds away on a shelf nearby.

"There he is," Nick said, catching sight of the pizza delivery car. A man was approaching from the street side. The guy had his head partly turned away from the camera while the conversation occurred between him and the driver. Money was exchanged before the man turned toward the camera, walking away from the vehicle and vanishing between two houses.

"That him?" he asked, freeze-framing the image on screen.

Alysia moved in closer to him, their shoulders touching. "No, that's not him," she said in a frustrated tone of voice. She cleared her throat. "He sent someone else in his place. I wonder how much that guy knows? Does he have any idea what Poe's capable of? He might be in danger as well. Someone should warn him."

"It does give us another lead. Nils can use face recognition technology — find out who he is. If he has a driver's license, he's on record." For a guy who was supposed to be so clever, why would he take the chance of having someone caught on video? Nick's stomach clenched into a fist. Yeah, things were escalating if he was willing to do something so foolish. Of course, Poe knew Alysia wouldn't go to the cops. But if something did happen to her — God forbid — then the images implicated him if a connection could be found between the two men. *So that means he's not worried about it. Thinks he's above the law and he's going to finish things.* Did he have an endgame? And how soon did he intend to introduce it? The image of sand pouring through an hourglass filled his mind. He kept all his suspicions to himself. The last thing he wanted was to upset Alysia any further.

"What's next?" she asked. "What do you need me to do?"

"I want you to sit tight until he's caught. That's the best thing you can do for me. For all of us. He's out there somewhere and we're going to get him. Hand him over to the authorities."

"But all he's done so far that we can prove is have someone put a note in a pizza box. It will just make him angrier. And the police can't hold him long for that."

"Oh, he's done far worse things than send threatening notes. I'm certain Nils will find enough evidence to charge him with multiple offenses. And if he's been doing what I think he's been doing all along, there will be a trail of evidence."

"You mean harming others? Women who were taken in my place."

"That's not on you. That's on him. He's a serial killer, for Christ's sake! And whether you existed or not, he'd still be doing the same thing. You have to believe that. *None* of this is on you."

She went quiet, staring at the image on the computer. *Why do victims blame themselves?* He felt helpless, wanting to reassure her more, make her feel right about things. But only time and patience could achieve that. He switched off the monitors.

She turned and kissed his cheek, pressing warm lips against his flesh, and it was his undoing. "Make love to me like it's our last time, Nick."

The simplicity of her message brought a sudden tear to his eye.

"Oh, beautiful," he murmured, pulling her into his arms. "Don't ever say that. I want to make love to you every day. All day. We've got all the time in the world, baby." He reassured her, but, still, he fully understood where she was coming from. She'd spent years and years watching over her shoulder, for the evil lurking in the background ready to pounce and destroy what she had built. Then he kissed her lips and forgot to think about anything but having her in his arms.

Their kiss was raw. So wonderfully raw. It spoke to him of her passion even as he tried to absorb her pain. He wanted to take away all her burdens. To help her release all the grief and hurt once and for all. To heal her mind and her soul. To enable her to live as she was meant to. There was so much he wanted for her and it drove his passion with the intensity of a thousand suns, searing him and strengthening his own inner mettle. He pulled back to kiss her cheeks, her neck, the skin above the neckline of her T-shirt, wanting to devour her. Keep her in his arms. Keep her safe forever.

He skimmed his hands up her body, her full breasts filling his palms. She moaned when he pinched her nipples between his thumb and forefinger. Reaching down, he yanked the top over her head and undid her bra. He leaned to suck one hardened bud into his mouth—sucked hard. Her body vibrated against his and music filled his mind and his soul.

"Yes!" she said, holding on to the back of his head with both hands, giving him access to whatever he wanted. It was everything he needed.

He undid the zipper on her jeans and tugged them off her legs, revealing her white lace panties. He made short work of the underwear, leaving her naked, a work of art, nature's finest creation. He picked her up and deposited her on the desk, pushing his computer and work aside. Spreading her legs, resting her ass cheeks against the bare wood, he admired the view while he hurried to tear off his own clothing and put on a condom.

He pulled her to the edge of the smooth surface, tight against him, and his cock nudged against the soft inner lips of her pussy. She was wet for him, *so beautifully wet*, and he slid in deep. Then deeper, until he was right up against her groin, right up against the heat radiating from her vibrating body…right up against heaven on earth. He ground himself into her, enjoying how she stretched for him, accommodated him. She made him feel more alive. More capable. *More everything.*

"*Oh yes!*" she encouraged him, pushing hard against him and giving as good as she got, raking his back lightly with her fingernails.

"Hang on, baby." He thrust, long moments of stroking in and out of her channel, until her muscles clenched and spasmed around his cock. When he could no longer hold back, he filled her with his heat and essence, collapsing against her. He held on to her, rocking her gently in his arms, reluctant to end this most precious of moments. The moment when he knew he was falling in love. Dizzy with excess emotion, he held on to her with all his might.

"I want to stay right like this forever," she murmured. The words made him smile. Yes, so did he.

His cell phone rang on his desk and he reluctantly pulled out of her tight body, then deposited the rubber in the trashcan beside the desk.

He picked up the phone and answered with one curt word, "Yes."

"Nick Wheeler?" an officious voice asked on the other end of the line.

"Speaking."

"This is the Grenville Island Detachment. We have a Walter Wheeler in custody. You're listed as his next of kin?"

His stomach made a sickening somersault. *What now?*

"Yes, I'm his grandson."

Alysia looked up from pulling on her underwear, her expression concerned.

"What's going on, Officer? Is my grandfather okay?"

"Yes, he's fine. But we need you to come by the station. Your grandfather was picked up earlier this evening for having drugs in his possession, but more concerning for us is his state of mind. Does he have dementia? He's exhibiting all the classic signs."

"It's never been confirmed by a doctor." Nick closed his eyes. No way would he lie about that. But he was filled with relief that the old man wasn't hurt. He chastised himself for not being there and keeping him from leaving the house. Not that he could chain him up. Walter did what Walter wanted to do, and to hell with everyone else.

"I'll be there shortly to pick him up." He pushed End and set the phone down.

"Will you be okay? I need to pick Walter up at the police station. It's close by. You can come with me."

"No. *Go.* I'll be fine. I want to take a shower anyway."

Nick pulled on his clothes and kissed her cheek. "I'll be back within the hour unless Walter pulls a fast one. The alarm system's on. Just stay away from the doors and windows. I really don't expect any more problems tonight. The creep's made his point."

"No problem. I want to call Kate again and check in with her. Then grab forty winks if you're not back, maybe on that cot in the safe room. I think a person could feel very secure in there."

"Sounds good. But the whole house is armed and damn near a fortress. Rest up. I intend to keep you up a good part of the night, beautiful."

"Only part? My, how the mighty have fallen." She gave him a wink, a soft smile lighting her face. He touched two fingers to his lips and threw her a kiss. She caught it and pressed it to her heart. His heart melted even further, if that was possible.

"Catch you later, beautiful. By the way, do you happen to like sex swings in the bedroom?" he found himself asking in the heat of the moment, adding what he hoped was a sexy leer. Talking about sex trumped everything else. And now he found he wanted to know every last thing about her. Especially what she wanted in the bedroom.

She caught the reference, her eyes widening with interest. "Enough to know that it just might be doable, handsome. Something a little extra to savor for a future date. What made you ask that?"

He liked the sound of that, *a future date*. "That first night, when you arrived on my doorstep, I had been dreaming of a naked woman who looked just like you sitting in one. Hot as Hades."

She smiled in that enigmatic way she had. Mona Lisa had nothing on her. And she was twice as beautiful. "I like the idea, very much," she purred.

Definitely my kind of woman.

Chapter Twenty

Alysia hurried upstairs to the second-floor bathroom. She tugged off her clothes and tossed them onto the counter. She had a shower, slowed down by thoughts of the night yet to come, dreaming of his touch, his lips on hers. Nick, of the strong hands and stronger promises. A man who could make her forget everything else when he was touching her.

Hmm, so a sex swing interests him. Her as well, if she was being honest. Her mind filled with the intriguing possibilities, giving her a mind-rush of monumental proportions. Anticipation, the fuel of great fantasies, kept her in its grip as she let the water pour over her, washing the day away.

She dried off. *Damn. No clean clothes.* They had to rectify that soon. At least she had another set of fresh underwear. And the knife she'd dug out of her work locker was strapped to her leg.

Dressed, she sat on the edge of the bed and gave Kate a call on the cell phone Nick had given her to replace her busted one. As she waited for her friend to pick up, she idly ran a fingertip over the shell of the device, remembering what he'd told her about its history. He'd explained it was a special one that Nils had provided, with graphene used not only for its touch pad, but also for its entire case. In essence, it was a battery capable of storing small amounts of electricity. She had always enjoyed physics and science, which had caused her to take an interest. He'd gone on to share that it would likely replace the fuel for cars one day, which sounded green and cool. Oh, and that the two guys who had discovered it had gotten Nobel Prizes for Physics. It had made her think of him as a James Bond character, which didn't hurt his cachet one bit.

Hmm. No answer except for the answering machine's impersonal message. Where was Kate? She sat and worried a thumbnail. Should she call BC-STAR? See if anything had happened? Indecisive, she sat and worried. She redialed. No answer. After the third try, she called the office. Maybe someone there knew something.

"BC-STAR, how may I help you?"

"Jaqueline, it's Alysia. Have you heard anything from Kate Baker? I can't reach her at home."

"Oh, yes, we were called out a couple of hours ago. She's been taken to Vancouver. I'm afraid she's had a setback—she was found unconscious. She's at Vancouver General. The crew on scene were able to stabilize her. I'm waiting to hear from them how she's doing. We're all worried, of course."

Alysia's heart squeezed tight in her chest, making it hard to take a full breath. "She sounded better earlier today," she said, her tone weakened by worry.

"I'm sorry — these things happen out of left field all the damn time. Cancer's a bitch. I have the number of the hospital here."

"Yes, I need it."

She grabbed a pen and scribbled down the numbers on a pad of paper sitting on the night table by the bed.

"Thanks, Jaqueline. You can reach me at this number if you need to." She recited the number of the cell phone to her friend. "I'm heading over to the hospital now. I'll let you know how she's doing soon as I can."

"Thanks. Oh, got to go, incoming."

They disconnected. She jumped up and raced from the room, all thoughts of a nap vanished. There was only one thought on her brain as she collected her borrowed winter jacket and ran to the garage. *Get to the hospital.* God, what if this was the last time she would ever see her dearest friend alive? The thought instilled fear into every cell in her body and made her pulse race with excess adrenaline, the edges of her vision narrowing and darkening with the overwhelming stress. The ups and downs of the last few days were taking their toll.

In the garage, she hit the electronic button that opened the overhead door and backed the Mercedes out onto the street. Within seconds she was on her way, not giving a care to the fact that her driver's license had burned along with everything else. Everything could wait.

Traffic was light and she made the hospital in less than half an hour without being stopped by the cops. Not bad considering how erratically she was driving, dodging in and out of traffic. Parking was always a bitch around hospitals, where there were never enough spaces allotted, and after a few frustrated minutes of driving in circles, she finally found a spot in the parking lot across the street.

Finding an assortment of coins and bills in a small box on the console between the seats, she grabbed it and stuffed the money into her pocket. She'd pay Nick back later. Thinking of Nick gave her pause. What would he think of her running out like that? He certainly wouldn't be happy about it. Well, there was no help for it. She had to come. And no way would anyone else know what she was up to. It was too random an event for that to have happened, surely?

She fed the meter at the parking lot's entrance with a few loonies and took the numbered paper tag back to the vehicle, laying it on the dash as directed before locking the car. The last thing she needed was to have the vehicle towed. She double-checked the locks, unable to help herself. Was paranoia setting in? She ignored the unsettling thought, instead gaining a better sense of security from the second series of answering beeps from the car that proved the locks had engaged. Threading the keys on the ring between her fingers like a weapon, she pulled the jacket up around her neck and hurried to cross the street at the designated crosswalk, swirls of icy snow slicking the pavement and licking the hot skin of her face.

Inside the hospital, she stamped her feet, knocking off the last traces of snow. While there was far less of the white stuff here than up in the mountains, the warmer weather made the roads icier and more treacherous.

"I'm here to see Kate Baker."

The receptionist gave her a quick look, then checked her computer screen. "Let's see. Yes, she's out of emergency and in room five-ten. You can take the elevator to your right."

She hurried in the direction the woman had pointed out, waiting impatiently for the doors to open. People streamed out of the tight space and she got in by herself, pressing the button to the fifth floor.

"Hold the doors, please," someone yelled. She did, wishing they'd hurry the hell up. A young couple got on and smiled at her. She found it hard to return the greeting. The doors closed and up they went with a sickening lurch of the mechanism.

The man and woman disembarked one floor before Kate's, and she tried to keep from screaming at them to hurry when they moved like snails. But finally the elevator began ascending again and she waited, her throat tightening, then got off on Kate's floor. Down the hallway she half-ran, checking the number on the walls by each doorway.

Room five-ten.

She came to a dead stop. She stood in front of the closed door. The fact that Kate was already in a room and not still in Emergency was a good sign, she reminded herself.

She pushed open the door and looked around the room, her head bobbing side to side. Two beds in the room, only one patient. Kate. She was being attended by a nurse. Alysia drew nearer and saw the moment her friend realized she was there for her. Her tired face gave a slight smile of greeting. She wore a colorful scarf on her head, bright pink today. It gave a little color to her pale cheeks. But her blue eyes looked tired and sad, like those of a woman pushing a huge boulder up an impossibly steep hill.

"Hey, girlfriend. What are you doing skiving off here?" Kate greeted her.

"I invited myself. What the hell are you doing here is more the question? You sounded pretty good earlier today. You decide you wanted to be waited on hand and foot again?"

Kate winced as the nurse probed her arm, trying to find a working vein. "Yeah, well, kind of nice. Better food, too."

Alysia snorted, not bothering to hide her complete indictment against hospital fare. Her scathing assessment was apparently also held by the nurse, who turned and gave her a look, adding a wink of understanding.

"If she hangs around 'til Friday, the lasagna's not bad," the nurse said. "Nearly recognizable."

Friday's three days away. Will she really still be in the hospital?

"Might be worth it," Kate said. "I'm a big fan of Italian food."

The nurse finished up and came closer to Alysia. "Don't tire her out. She needs her rest."

"I understand. I won't stay long."

She gave her friend a kiss on the cheek, then pulled up a chair.

"They want me to go into hospice care," Kate said, picking at her covers, breaking off a bit of thread from the machine stitching on the sheet.

Alysia swallowed, trying to imagine herself in the same situation. It was impossible, try as she might. She was too strong, too alive to pull on the mantle of being so deadly ill.

"Can you stay in your own home with more help? I could move in with you," she said.

Kate was silent for a moment. "Much as I appreciate the offer, you've got your own problems. Living with a woman who's only going to get sicker? It isn't going to be much fun. The loss of consciousness was brought on by the cancer spreading. The old noggin is now affected." Kate tapped a finger against the side of her head.

Alysia took her friend's hands in her own, absorbing the bad news but not willing to give up. "I'm not worried about it being fun, I'm only worried about you."

"Hey, we'll always have Disneyland. Remember Christmas Day and there was hardly anyone else around? No lines for any of the rides." Kate began coughing, her pale face turning an alarming shade of red. That vacation together had been two years ago. With neither of them having parents, they'd decided to spend the difficult holiday together at the happiest place on Earth. It had worked, being caught up in the fantasy. Last Christmas they'd chosen Las Vegas and attended a variety of shows. Soon after that, Kate had gotten sick. Would her friend still be around for next Christmas? The thought chilled her to the bone. It was looking less and less likely.

Alysia patted her back. "Water?" she asked.

Kate nodded.

It took a few minutes, but finally her body quieted and she slumped back against the white pillow case. Alysia tucked the covers around her friend and sat. She spied the open paperback on the side table. Her friend always had a historical romance on the go, saying the thoughts of another time and era took her mind away.

"You want me to read to you?"

"Maybe later. I want you to tell me all about this new guy in your life. Come on, spill. You know you want to.

I've never seen you look better. You getting it regular already?"

Alysia blushed. "We hardly know each other."

"*Phhht*. Like that matters," Kate scoffed. "A woman knows these things right off the hop."

"He's been a lot of help. Makes me feel safe," she admitted.

"That's good. Safe and horny, eh?"

"Yeah, maybe." She gave a small chuckle, not meeting her friend's eyes. "He's connected to a good group of people that like to help others. They call themselves TETRAD."

"I'm happy for you. If I were you, I'd be grabbing at this opportunity with both hands."

"We'll see. I've got a lot on my mind right now. No time for romance."

"Always time for romance." Kate suddenly looked exhausted.

"You want me to read to you now?"

"No, I think I need to close my eyes for a bit."

"Okay. I'll wait while you go to sleep." She was in no rush to leave, finding solace in Kate's company.

"You should go home. I'll still be here tomorrow. I promise."

"I'll leave in a bit."

Alysia pulled her phone out of her pocket, noting the low battery signal. She quickly texted Nick to let him know the deal. The last thing she wanted was him arriving home and finding her gone.

She waited, listening to her friend's soft intake of breaths. She didn't want to look ahead to the future. Not yet.

Chapter Twenty-One

"So help me, Walter, if you don't quit pulling this stupid shite, I won't be held responsible for my actions." Nick raked a hand through his hair. Frustrated and annoyed didn't begin to cover it. It had taken the better part of two hours cooling his heels on a bench in the visitors' section, but finally his grandfather, led by a concerned police officer, had stumbled out into the waiting area. Walter's bewilderment act was firmly in play, of course.

Nick turned his head now as he drove to give his passenger the full range of his annoyance in a scorching look meant to quell the old man's rebellion. At least long enough to gain some peace while he worked to reconnect with Alysia.

"Where we headed?" Walter asked.

"Vancouver General."

"Why? You sick or something?"

"I should be getting *you* checked out. At least that's what the officer advised," Nick said, pushing the SUV to the limits, dodging around traffic. What had that woman been thinking? Leaving on her own without an escort? Without him at her side to guarantee her safety?

"What do they know?" Walter scoffed, looking like he was about to launch into one of his famous tirades against *The Man*. "Always trying to keep society from having a good time. It's only those that stand to gain something from controlling us that thinks they are in charge, sonny boy. From the law to the priests, it's all about us working for *them*. Controlling us. A man dares to think for himself, lord help him, and he's inundated with all kinds of bullshit."

"Thinking for yourself always seems to involve drugs with you. Hard to follow that logic when drugs are another trap of mankind."

"Hmph. At least it's one of my own choosing. One I'm willing to pay for."

"Well, keep it up and you know where you're headed, right? This is your final warning. I can't keep covering for you."

"An old man asking for a little peace in his old age. Fucking ingrate society. And after a man does his sworn duty to his country." Walter shook his head with disgust, his face twisted in a scowl. "You know your grandmother and me married after knowing each other only three days, right? That what's going on here? You running after that girl?"

Nick felt punched in the solar plexus with the idea coming so far out of left field. Trust Walter to stir things up. He took a deep breath and made himself answer in a calmer tone of voice. "It was a different time with the war going on. Lots of people married too soon and spent years, hell, decades, regretting it."

"Nothing to regret. Lots of us made it long term. Don't be such a pompous jackass. Besides, you two got your own personal war going on. Grab what you can *when* you can, that's my best advice. Regret getting married — my ass. I worshiped that woman. She was everything to me. Don't be telling me about how long you need to know someone before you damn well know the score."

Thankfully his grandfather fell into another sulk, leaving him in silence.

His chest tightened. What if Alysia had been followed to the hospital? Was she even now in mortal danger? In the clutches of a madman? *Christ, what is taking so long?* He wanted to knock all the fucking traffic right out of the way with a bulldozer, but settled for laying on the horn. Good and loud.

Then it happened.

The driver in the car ahead of him slammed on their brakes and the SUV slid right into the back of them. *CRASH.* The screech of brakes, metal and plastic colliding resounded. Not with enough force to make the airbags deploy, but enough to bring traffic to a dead standstill in their lane.

"Jesus fucking Christ!"

"Great job." His grandfather shook his head, making Nick see a haze of red. He closed his eyes for a second, desperate to keep himself together. This was not the time to lose it. Alysia needed him.

"Stay here. Pretend you're not feeling well. That should be easy." He jumped out and rushed to the driver's window of the older-model sports car. Peered inside. Just one person at the wheel.

He gestured impatiently for the older man, who looked to be in his seventies or eighties, to roll down his window. The guy gave him a frown before finally complying.

"You okay?" Nick asked.

"Yeah, think so. How badly hurt's my baby?"

Nick gave a startle, his heart thudding loudly. "Baby? What baby?"

"My Mazda RX7. I've had her since nineteen eighty-three. Got her brand-new. For my fortieth birthday. A classic car. Going to be hard to fix it if there's much damage. Parts are hard to come by, you know, all the way from Japan if you can get them. Here, let me get out."

Nick groaned inside. Just what he needed. He looked up at the heavens and shook his head when what he really wanted to do was shake his fist. *Why today? When I most need to be somewhere?*

He stepped back and let the guy out of the driver's door. He followed the stooped man around to the back of the silver vehicle. He bit his lip, drawing blood, to keep himself from screaming profanities.

"Oh, dear. This doesn't look good at all." The man shook his head back and forth, a forlorn expression coming over his face. "Sorry, girl, I shouldn't have taken you out of the garage on such a day as this. All my fault." The man rubbed the back fender of the car, noting the damage, his eyes tearing up in the process.

"Can we exchange cards and get a move on? I'll pay for all the damages, but I'm on my way to the hospital." He nodded toward Walter in the SUV. "My grandfather, he needs to get there right away. I think he's having a heart attack." And if Walter wasn't, his grandson was.

"Oh my. But don't we have to wait for the cops? I mean, I'm not sure. Your grandfather, you say? I guess you'd better go. Or we could call an ambulance? Then we can wait for the cops."

"No, I have to go with him. He's all alone in the world. You understand. We just lost my parents and he's still upset." Nick wanted to shut it down, feeling like the lowest of the low for using his parents. But he knew they'd understand. They'd had a love affair that would have caused them to act the same, one for the other. He ignored the thought of calling his current situation a love affair and instead concentrated on getting to where he needed to be.

"Oh, of course." The man dug out a tattered white card with great difficulty from his wallet and handed it to Nick, who made a valiant effort not to snatch it right out of the man's hands.

"Here's mine. And five hundred dollars for your trouble." He pulled out most of his walking-around money and handed it to the rather nice but slightly bewildered man. "Thank you for your understanding. I'll pay whatever it costs. This is just the down payment in the spirit of goodwill." He read the name on the business card. "George McPherson. Thanks, George. I'll call you first thing in the morning and we can straighten it all out."

He gave the man a solid look and shook his proffered hand. He raced back to his SUV, grateful it was still in running order. He pulled out around the RX7 and into the flow of traffic. His nerves twitched and his head ached with the effort to hold it together. To floor the gas pedal and to hell with everything else. But there was no point in having a second accident in one night. Finally, when he was certain he was going to lose it, the big H that designated hospitals appeared on a traffic sign and he pulled into the proper lane to access it.

He double-parked in front of the hospital, leaving the motor running. "Wait here. Move it if you have to."

Without waiting for an answer, he jumped out and tore off toward the hospital entrance. The electric doors slid open on a soft hiss and he raced through them. His heartbeat pounding in his ears making his mind near explode with white noise, he ran full bore toward the reception desk.

"Kate Baker," he barked, showing his credentials supplied by the company. "It's an emergency." The woman started, but blessed him with a quick answer.

"Room five-ten. Should I call security?" she asked, reaching for the phone.

"No, not yet. I need to see if she's there first. If she is, everything will be fine."

He took off at a fast clip, made the elevators in a few strides and punched in the correct floor number. *Please, please, dear God, let her be there,* he prayed.

He stepped off the elevator and ran the final few paces to Kate's room. Pushed open the door with a shove and hurried inside. He gave a quick look around, his bloody head spinning with the pressure of needing to know. Of praying she was right here. *Please God.* He swallowed. No answer for all his pleading today.

The room was empty. Except for the young woman fast asleep in the hospital bed.

Oh, Christ, no. He swallowed past the huge lump growing in his throat then heard a slight noise in the adjoining room. His interest zeroed in on it. He strode over to the bathroom and caught sight of Alysia running water in the sink. She looked up at him, startled by his abrupt appearance.

"Nick," she said, setting aside a vase of flowers she had been topping up with the water. She gave him a smile. The sweetest smile of his whole life. Relief filled him. He strode over to her and grabbed onto her, his heart still pounding.

"Thank you, God," he said, wrapping his arms around her.

They hugged. He took a deep, cleansing breath. Then righteous anger filled him and he pulled back from her. "What the hell were you thinking, taking off like that?"

"Lower your voice. Kate's sleeping." She gave him a stern look, her voice tightly controlled. She took a step back as well. "I'm perfectly fine. I'm not a damn prisoner, you know. My friend needed me and I came. Isn't that why you left me a vehicle for me to use? I texted you I was here," she hissed.

He bit his lip. "No, you're not a prisoner. But you had me scared out of my wits. If anything had happened to you—" He couldn't go there. He wasn't wrong about her making a huge mistake by not waiting until she had him to accompany her. He had to tell her more about what Nils had discovered. *Now.* Before she made any more damn mistakes that could have far-reaching consequences.

"There are things you need to know. Information that's just come to light." It was hard to whisper when he wanted to shout. Feeling hamstrung by being in the hospital and by circumstance just upped his anger quotient. His skin literally itched from the pressure. He felt stripped bare.

"What things?" She narrowed her eyes at him as if he were the bad guy. He tried not to take offense but she wasn't making it easy. *So be it.* She had to know.

"There are two other victims with the MO of Edgar Allan Poe quotes left at the scenes of their capture—the car park at the library and outside the coffee shop. Both within the last six weeks. Two young women about your age, size and build. Similar hair and facial features."

He hesitated before deciding not to tell her that their bodies had been dropped off at a local area hospital with instructions to use their fresh parts for organ transplant. Something that had law enforcement in an uproar. The perp was wanting to go down in the annals of history as an evil villain without any semblance of humanity left in him. It sickened him more than he could say and was more proof that Poe had fallen right into the deep end with his insanity. How much was Poe? And how much was his brain injury? About now he didn't care—he just wanted the fucker gone. Every trace of him scoured from the face of the planet.

He continued with just the pertinent facts, "Cryptic notes were left on their vehicle's dash for law enforcement to find."

She froze, her expression horrified.

"Another thing. He's more erratic because he experienced brain damage in the accident, to his frontal lobe. The part that controls emotions. He's never been more dangerous, Alysia, and here you are just acting like a damn idiot racing all over the place without protection. Without giving me the opportunity to make certain you're safe." He hadn't meant to say so much, but it spilled out of him. His tone had increased in volume as well, making her wince.

A weak voice came through the doorway. "Everything okay in there?"

"Great. Now you've woken Kate. You should go," she said. She picked up the vase of red roses, her expression cold and distant. Like she'd shut everything down behind those eyes that normally shone with such clarity. *Christ. Is that my fault too?*

"Those were my mother's favorite." A prickling behind his eyes took him by surprise. He hid it by leaning down and breathing in the intoxicating fragrance of the flowers. He was off balance and he knew it. *Keep it together, Nick.*

"I'm going to stay with Kate until she goes to sleep — again. Then I'll drive myself home." She didn't wait for an answer but stepped around him and went to her friend. Nick took a deep breath and stared at his reflection in the mirror. He looked haunted. He turned on the taps and splashed his face then picked up a towel from the rack to dry off.

Now what? He had Walter outside, fuming no doubt, and a woman who would not see reason in the other room. What the hell was this day coming to? Was it just a few hours ago he'd held her in his arms, made love to her? Now everything was fucked up beyond recognition. He'd let his anger get the better of him. One of his traits, if he were being honest.

He'd joined TETRAD to try to do good in the world. Straighten out problems that threatened to overwhelm people. How could this one have gone so far off the rails? Especially when it had never mattered more to him to keep someone safe from harm. Was it him? Was he wrong to want to keep her safe? She had done a pretty good job up until now. That said a lot. But things had changed. That was what she didn't get. Poe was more dangerous now than ever. He had plans. Horrifying plans. And they included Alysia.

No. I'm right. He had to take a hard stance. It was for her own good. Even if it meant she never forgave him. Bile scorched the back of his throat. Her safety mattered more to him than anything. He wanted her to have a good life, *hell*, have a chance at a life. And if he had to give her up to make her see reason, to let him keep her safe while he took out the bad guy, so be it. He would do anything it took to make sure she lived another day. But what he wouldn't give to have her in his life for all their days. *Yeah, Walter, you're right about one thing — marrying Grandma after only three days of knowing her makes a whole lot of sense now. Even if it was wartime.* Because this too was war. A war against evil.

Chapter Twenty-Two

Alysia set the flowers by Kate's bed. She gave her friend a smile she didn't feel. She was beyond angry. *How dare he!* And, God, to think there had been two other victims. He'd just dropped it on her. Used them to prove his case. Well, she'd kept herself safe up until now. She'd continue to do so. She was no babe in the woods. Her world was imploding and she fell back on the only way she knew how to be. *Independent and unfeeling.*

"Everything all right?" Kate looked at her. "I heard arguing."

"I'm sorry we woke you. It's Nick. He's in the bathroom. We had a disagreement."

"You want to talk about it?"

She shook her head. "Nothing to say really. He wants to keep me a prisoner and I want my freedom."

"I think he just wants you to be safe, right? Did coming to the hospital tonight put you at risk?" Her tired blue eyes filled with instant worry.

"No, of course not! I always take precautions, you know that." The last thing she wanted was Kate to blame herself for anything. The very idea filled her with even more righteous anger.

Nick finally came out of the bathroom, but she studiously ignored him.

He took command of the room, his voice fueled by a cold force that vibrated within her, making him impossible to totally ignore. Whether she liked it or not, he was getting to her on some elementary level she didn't have complete control over. Yet. "I'm going to move my vehicle, then come back and escort you safely to yours." He didn't wait for an answer but strode officiously from the room.

"I'd say you might have pissed him off a tad," Kate said, giving her a crooked smile.

She didn't say anything but fiddled some with the roses. They were Kate's favorite. Hers too if she were being honest. But no one had ever bought her flowers. Of course, she'd never really had a boyfriend. Just hookups. It was safer, especially for them. But things were changing with Nick. Would he still be around once Poe was caught? Did she want him to be? Not at the moment she didn't, even though she had enjoyed spending time with him up until now, even under horrendously difficult circumstances. He was making her life more bearable at times, pushing aside the usual bullshit that had consumed her for years. Why did he have to go and ruin that? Act like such a dork? Make her want to strangle him with her bare hands?

"Don't worry about it. You want me to read to you?"

"Please."

She picked up the paperback, turned to the page with the bookmark and began reading. At least it would be something to take her mind off today. She couldn't think about the other victims. Not yet. It was too raw, too real, and it threatened to overwhelm what little sanity she had left.

She read but was unable to follow the story. A few minutes later she looked up and realized Kate had fallen asleep.

She leaned down and kissed her friend's forehead.

"Sleep well. I'll be back tomorrow," she whispered. She pressed her lips together to keep from crying. She turned and walked away quickly, joining Nick, who waited, lurking, in the hallway. She spared him a quick glance. He looked more composed, as if the walk outside into the cold had done him some good.

"Okay. I'll walk you to the car, then drive Walter home. Damn fool, getting himself arrested again."

"No need. I have my pepper spray and my keys I always keep threaded through my fingers. Handy weapon in a pinch. You drive your grandfather home and I'll meet you there. It's almost midnight." She didn't mention the knife strapped to her lower calf. That was her secret alone. She needed the sense of security it gave her. Though she'd taken an oath to save victims of accidents and crimes, that didn't mean she had to become one herself by not defending herself. She'd always vowed to go down fighting.

"Sorry. Not letting you out of my sight. You had me tied up in knots, you know, thinking of all the horrid things that could have happened to you on the drive over. Then I ran into the back of this poor old guy, hurt his prized sports car."

"You had an accident? You and Walter okay?" *You'd think he would have mentioned that sooner*, she fumed. He must have been even more worried about her than he'd let on, and he'd let on plenty.

"Just a fender bender. Nothing serious. But it held me up."

The elevator let them off at the lobby. But as soon as they walked out of the front entrance, she spotted a security cop nosing around the SUV parked in one of a handful of easy-access metered stalls near the front entrance. Now what was his grandfather up to?

"You'd better drive Walter home—looks like he's been busy. I'm right over there." She pointed out the black car clearly visible under the bright lights of the car park. "Just across the street. I've got my pepper spray handy. I'll meet you at the house." She hurried away before Nick could object. He had his hands full and didn't need to be her nursemaid. She'd done for herself for years now. And she was still standing, unbeholden to any man.

She was halfway across the street when Nick caught up to her. Without saying a word, he strode by her side. It was a short distance to her parked vehicle, a matter of less than a minute. He gave a visual check of the interior, then stood and watched while she unlocked it with the keys she'd threaded between her fingers. She opened the driver's door and slid in behind the wheel.

"See you back at the house." His tone was cool and she didn't bother to answer him, just gave a curt nod. *Keep it professional. It'll hurt less when this is all over.* Because it was becoming obvious they were not compatible. Not when he wanted to control her every action. *Not going to happen, buddy. Not now, not ever.*

She gave a careful look around as Nick walked away, but nothing was amiss in the parking garage. Open to the street, but covered overhead, the large complex let in the cold while providing some cover from the elements. She took a deep breath, happy to be safely locked inside. She started the motor and drove around to the side entrance on the east side that also served as the exit. Alysia punched in the code on her ticket and waited for the metal door arm to go upwards to allow her to leave. But though she did it twice, nothing happened. *Damn it.*

She peered at the toll shack to see if an operator was available. Often, after a certain hour, a customer was on their own, but, tonight, the small booth was lit up inside. *Thank goodness.*

She laid on the horn, hoping the attendant would come out and give her a hand. Nothing happened. Frustrated, she tried the code again. Nothing. *Shit.*

Nothing else for it but to get out and check in with the operator.

She reluctantly got out of the car and looked around. *Not a soul in sight. Figures.* Well, better that than someone right behind her blasting their horn at her to make her move faster. *Never helps.* She strode toward the small building to her left, her snow boots making small scuffling sounds on the pavement. She knocked on the narrow door with the glass insert to get the attendant's attention. He was turned away from her, slumped against the counter. *Was he sleeping? Drunk? Having a health emergency?*

She knocked a second time. Louder. Her knuckles stung as she rapped them against the icy-cold metal. Footfalls drew her attention behind her. She knocked louder, pounding at the door, then in the next second whirled around, fear flooding her system. Someone was close. Too close, in her personal space. She knew at that exact second even as the face registered in her brain. *Evil.* Evil had come for her.

Serendipity. Obviously, someone was smiling down on him today. The gods of his imagination were the gods of chaos. He no more believed in a benign God than did his hero, Edgar Allan Poe, who was not above expressing his dislike of organized religion. The celebrated author who understood the dark side of mankind didn't believe in the concept of God, at least not the kind to just lead him right to his heart's desire. His prey. There she was. Alysia. Walking. Talking. She left the asshole at the front entrance then came across the street right toward him, as though she was embracing her new dark lover.

His breath stilled. *Shit.* The asshole was rejoining her. Bloody hell. The fucker just didn't get it. Sure, he could keep her safe one more day, but he'd get to her. No fucking doubt about that. With grim determination, he watched Wheeler escort her across the street to her vehicle, expecting him to get inside and drive her home. But all he did was give the Mercedes a quick check and let her drive away alone. *Too perfect.*

He was prepared. It had been so easy. Make her friend ill enough to be rushed to the hospital. The beauty of GHB or gamma hydroxybutyric acid or one of the so-called date rape drugs? It came in many forms. One just perfect for his needs. A nice spray mist or a powder to mix in to a favorite drink of 'Kate the Friend'.

And it had been just as easy to slip into the toll booth earlier. Its location on the side street made him less visible to traffic. When the man in charge of collecting the money for tickets had turned to check him out, he'd sprayed the fine mist from his reverse-engineered e-cigarette directly into his face. He enjoyed the image of an Amazonian tribesman doing the same with a poisoned dart gun. The victim had fallen forward. He'd righted the body, turning it away from view of those leaving the car park.

He'd then disarmed the electronic mechanism to open the gate. He'd manned the booth, slipping inside every time a customer needed to leave. He'd pressed the lever only available to the operator, raising the bar and waving them through, then slipped back out and hid behind a pillar to watch for her. Waited. All a matter of superb timing really. *Damn, I'm good.* A brilliant machine housed in muscle and bone.

Now she was so nearby he could taste her. *Taste her fear.* It made him forget his damn aching head for seconds at a time. He watched her drive up to the armed gate a couple of minutes later. Key in the code. Then do it again. What was the definition of insanity credited to Einstein in most people's books, that overused cliché about doing the same action again and expecting a different outcome? *Not going to work for you today, Alysia. Sorry about that.*

He waited until she began to knock on the office door. Perfect. No one around. The time was now.

When she whirled around to discover who had come up behind her, he sprayed the fine mist into her face, his own carefully covered by a doctor's mask, certainly garb expected at a hospital. At the library he'd used a breathing apparatus, like a dutiful worker using solvent to clean the stone.

He grabbed her as she slumped forward. He dragged her the short distance to his van, opened the back door and shoved her inside. He strode back to her car and got into the driver's seat. Again, fate was shining on him. Nobody was waiting to exit. He allowed himself a small smile. His actions truly were blessed today. He backed up the compact Mercedes and parked it where it wouldn't be noticed right away. Locking it with her key fob, he hurried back to his own vehicle. Seconds later he ripped off the white paper mask, tossing it onto the seat beside him, and drove off the lot. *Mission accomplished.*

Nick hurried back to Walter and the SUV. The security cop was gone now. One small fact in his grandfather's favor.

He climbed into the vehicle and started the motor, leaving it to idle, climate change or no climate change. He wanted to be able to take off at a moment's notice. A couple of minutes slipped by. There was very little traffic in the area with it being so late, making it easy to watch for her. At least the hospital allowed visitors to the very ill pretty much around the clock. But tomorrow he'd be escorting her highness. No ifs, and or buts about it.

"What are we waiting for, the damn sun to come up?" Walter asked, his tone grumpy and out of sorts.

"You saying it's my fault your being out so late?" Nick turned and shot the comment at his passenger.

"Hmph." But at least his grandfather settled down, pressing his lips tightly together.

"I'm waiting for Alysia to exit the car park, if you must know. What's taking so damn long?" He kept an eye on the spot where she should be exiting, having watched her pull out of the parking space across from them a good few minutes ago.

"Maybe the vehicle had mechanical problems?" Walter suggested, making Nick roll his eyes in exasperation.

"Not bloody likely. That's a brand-new vehicle, recently serviced. Fully gassed up and ready to go. Chances of it stalling are nearly zero."

"Then what's the holdup? I gotta get to bed. Take my heart medicine."

"I'll check. Wait here."

"Huh, like I was going to get out. Friggin' cold enough to freeze the brass balls off a monkey. Why, with my—"

Nick closed the driver's door, stopping the tirade about his grandfather's perfectly good health in its tracks. His idea of 'heart medicine' was a vitamin pill, Nick knew.

He strode quickly across the street and under the canopy of the parking lot. No sign of Alysia or the car. What the fuck? *There.* He finally spotted it, parked in a different spot from before. He went to the vehicle and found it locked. *Damn it.* But on the dash was something that sent fear shuddering straight into his chest. A note. He tried to read it through the glass, but the print was too small. He'd need his extra set of keys from the house. Frustrated, he punched the window and ignored the pain. Where was she? There was the one way in and out of the lot. The booth was lit. He ran full speed across the cement floor, pounded on the metal door and yelled, "Let me in! Now!"

No answer.

He twisted the handle and the door swung open, squeaking on its hinges. Slumped on the narrow counter was the attendant. Nick took a couple of fast steps over to the man, placed his fingers on the man's cool neck, checking for a pulse. A weak heartbeat, but he was still breathing. He pulled out his cell phone and punched in nine-one-one, giving the location to the operator while ignoring the demand for his name. He didn't want to be tied up with the fallout from this situation. He had to find Alysia. Now. There was no time to waste.

He felt bad leaving the man, but there was no other choice. And help was just across the street. He was luckier than most. He ran full bore back to the SUV and jumped inside.

"Hang on. Poe's got Alysia. We're going after them."

"How? Where? There's no one around."

"If they didn't drive by us, then he had to have headed north. Back towards Hope is my bet."

"We're going back to Hope at this time of the night?"

"You want out?" Nick asked. He had no patience left. His last nerve had been scraped raw, laid bare by a madman. A madman who had the woman he realized had worked her way into his heart in the past forty-eight hours. A woman he wanted in his life. Permanently. He'd already waited a lifetime for a woman like her. Strong. Feisty. Confident. And now she was in mortal danger. On his watch. Anger tunneled his vision.

"I'm fine."

"Good. Hang on."

And that was all the words that were spoken between them for a long while. Meanwhile, he called his team and explained the situation in all its gory detail.

"Nils, I need a location on Poe. How close are you to having the coordinates?"

Nils answered his question in a hoarse tone of voice, having just woken up to answer the call.

"Working on it. Hedging the bets between land titles and an IP address. The bastard's stayed offline. What's happened?"

"He's taken her."

"Poe? Christ, okay, I'm on it. I'll call you back soon as I have anything."

Please, please let him find the location before we get to Hope. The window of time that existed for finding a victim of crime alive lit up with huge red numerals in the corner of his mind. *Tick. Tick. Tick.* It squeezed and constricted his chest in octopus-like tentacles growing ever tighter, making it near impossible to take a full breath. The first critical twenty-four hours were their best shot at getting Alysia back safely and they would slip by all too soon. Nick began praying like he'd never prayed before.

Chapter Twenty-Three

Day Three

She struggled, unable to find her way out. Was she underwater? Frightened. Nauseated. And unable to understand what was going on. *But then how can I breathe?*

When she finally came back to full consciousness a few shattering minutes later, she realized she had been asleep, her mind a kaleidoscope of swirling, disjointed images. Her dreams had been filled with impossible-to-understand vignettes of demons and angels fighting it out on some other world.

Then she was struck with an avalanche of excruciating pain when she dared open her eyes. *Where the fuck am I?* Fear crept in as the jumbled images from the car park loomed larger. *Oh My God.* Her mind realized what had happened a second before she fully understood. She threw up the contents of her stomach on the floor over the side of the cot she lay on.

She wiped her mouth with her sleeve and sat up. The stink of sickness permeated the air. She slumped back against the corrugated wall. No choice really, she was so damn weak. The sound caused a new noise and she looked down at her legs. *Oh God.* One ankle was chained. The tether was anchored in the wall, giving her about twelve feet of leeway. She pulled at it, but it was firmly attached to the steel wall.

She took a careful look around, slowly, because even her eyeballs hurt. They thudded with pain. But at least she was still wearing her glasses, smeared as they were. She took them off and cleaned them clumsily with the hem of her tee in efforts to see her surroundings more clearly.

The space was rudimentary. A twenty-foot-by-eight-foot room with about the same height of ceiling, it was made entirely of rusted metal. A shipping container like those designed for a cargo ship or train. It was lit with a few exposed electric bulbs overhead, its only furnishings the cot she sat on, a few blue water jugs piled in the corner, a chemical toilet and a basin with a roll of paper towels set up to the side. A quote was painted on one wall in black lettering, large enough to be read from where she sat. *The boundaries which divide Life from Death are at best shadowy and vague. Who shall say where one ends, and where the other begins?*

She shuddered at the concept. She had no doubts. She was alive. Knew the difference from her varied experiences as a nurse. *Poe.* She'd never let him fuck with her mind, with her version of reality any more than he already had done. The monster of her dreams had brought her here. And her hubris had allowed it to happen. Thinking she was the one in charge while he had known all along that it was an illusion. That he would get to her.

She let loose a huge sigh of anguish at her predicament. Holding her head in her hands, she pressed tightly against her temples. Why had she not listened to Nick? Because her friend had needed her. And she'd do it again but just change one thing — drive home with him and Walter and leave the damn car that represented freedom in the car park. Because freedom was an illusion that could get people killed. She knew her hours were numbered and, apparently, he intended to torture her first, or why was she still alive?

Her stomach clenched and heaved again at the horror of that realization, but all that came up this time was a stream of yellow bile. But she threw up again and again until her stomach was clenching painfully, fist-like, on its own emptiness. The dry heaves. She wiped her mouth with a trembling hand. She did feel a bit better having released the stress.

Then the memory of her six-inch knife strapped to her leg focused all her thoughts. She felt for the weapon under her jeans. It was still there, hidden next to her upper calf. *YES*. Hope filled her with an edgy sense of cold anticipation. She was armed. Ready to do battle. And if she was going down, so was he. She checked her pockets and found her phone there as well. Probably left because the battery was dead. She tossed it away with disgust. Knowing Poe, he'd done it to make her feel even more upset each time she looked at it and couldn't call for help. Devious fucking bastard.

But first she needed to clean up the floor. The disgusting smell of vomit was making her ill again. She pulled her ponytail tighter and re-fastened a couple of bobby pins to keep the hair out of her face, then bent to the task, to hide the evidence away in a covered trash container she found under the cot.

Poe watched the sunrise from his deck, bundled up in a winter coat and warming his hands around a cup of strong coffee. It was a glorious morning, the sun streaking across the sky in a riot of color. It was going to be a fine day. He thought of his prize buried thirty meters to his right. It had been costly to bury the shipping containers, but worth it. They were impossible to detect with the naked eye.

He had never felt more powerful. He'd stolen her right out from under their stupid noses. It was shocking how easy it had been, really. *Hmm.* Now the games could begin. He'd give her a choice — that was always such a sweet way to play it. The illusion of control. It worked with two-year-old children, and worked just as well with adults.

He drank the last of his coffee and went back inside to rinse the cup. Time to pay his guest a visit. A sudden blinding pain in his brain stopped him in his tracks and he rubbed at his forehead with a trembling hand. He hated the sign of weakness. The debilitating effects of the accident were not improving. If anything, they were getting more frequent. Doctors had said it was just a matter of time until the aneurism let go and he was annihilated. *But please, not today.* Not when he finally had her in his grasp.

He sank to his knees, waiting, hoping the fucking death grip would move off one more time. *Just a few more days. That's all I need. Payback for my life. And all I've lost.*

After a time, the pain eased and he got to his feet. He lurched to the door and out into the frosty morning. He shambled the short distance to the large machine shed that contained his tools. Opening the main door, he slipped inside and walked over to the north wall. He reached down and pressed an electrical switch on the underside of a portable bench, activating a hidden winch. The unit covered in tools moved forward on the floor, revealing the entrance to the two shipping containers he'd buried underground using a rented bulldozer. It had been a huge undertaking, but not uncommon in this part of the country where people wanted secret caverns for raising crops, some legal, some not—though that was mostly a thing of the past now that weed was legal in Canada.

He took the built-in ladder down to the first container, careful to reset the switch to cover the entrance once he was safely inside. He knew it was near to impossible to detect from topside once the cover was back in position. The security of knowing that was worth all the hours of hard labor creating the structure.

The space he entered was set up with a few more amenities than the one he'd placed Alysia in. A hot plate, portable fridge, working sink, coffee machine and a food cupboard along with a gravity-feed shower stall, composting toilet and toiletry goods—enough supplies for many months lined the walls. If she was a good guest, she'd keep the right to make use of it all. The next few minutes would tell the tale. He went to work, turned on the overhead fan and fired up the hotplate, preparing to make eggs for her breakfast. He'd give her the benefit of the doubt until she proved different. And if he had to recycle her for the benefit of the world, he'd do it. Her choice.

When he'd finished, he checked the computer monitor showing the live feed from the cameras located around her room. She was sitting on the cot, looking calm. *Good.* It was a start.

He took a deep breath. The pain in his head had receded to a dull thud, seeming to be keeping time with the blood in his veins. That was about the best he could hope for these days. He loathed it when it muddled his thinking, which it was doing more and more of late. He unlocked the door and stepped inside the room. She got up immediately, started towards him. Ah, but she wouldn't get far with that leg-iron.

He set the plate down and put up a warning hand armed with the e-cigarette holder pointed right at her. "Don't come too close or I will have to spray you again. You'll be out like a light for hours and wake up with another blaring headache."

She hesitated. Her large eyes were expressive in their deliberations. One thing he'd always liked about her even as a child, before all the shit began—she was intelligent. Understood things. Not as brilliant as himself, of course, no one was, but certainly a worthy female.

"How could you do this after I saved your life?" she hissed at him.

"My life wouldn't have been in danger if you hadn't been running all over hell's half-acre looking after that friend of yours. And what's the point? She'll be dead soon anyway. Logic dictates the inevitable. Stage four cancer, right?" He saw he'd scored a point as she blinked, her eyes reddened and watery. "You were to blame for my accident. Stands to reason you had to do what you did. And didn't you sign up for that anyway, as a trauma nurse?"

"Why are you doing this?" she asked, confusion obvious in her expression. She stood still facing him, the e-cigarette the only thing separating them. He watched her fingers flexing as if she itched to do something. *Just try it.* He had lightning-fast reflexes and he outweighed her by a good sixty pounds, mostly hard muscle.

He shrugged. "There are only three avenues open to immortality for humans. And since I'm obviously not going to be resurrected for the soul-narrative—not being the new messiah—it will have to be the legacy-narrative through deeds, foul or otherwise. Only way to bring myself into the future, unless you want to carry my progeny, my personal DNA and help me advance my personal genetics into the future? That's the third way and the one chosen by the majority of humans. Too soon in our evolution for data streams of our human genome to guarantee our essence continuing indefinitely. And freezing your head? That's ludicrous."

She stood, staring at him. Had he grown three legs? Horns? Did no one read anymore?

Well, no matter. But the third option made him ponder, especially the more he looked at her. She was a beautiful woman, no doubt about it. But was she the right one? *Hmm.* Maybe it wasn't too late for that option. Something stirred in him, a seed planting itself.

"Eat. Your food's getting cold." He backed out of the room and slammed the door shut, locking it. He sat on the stool in front of the camera that showed the full expanse of Alysia's room. Time to watch. Figure out her mindset. Exploit her psychology before her physiology. Given sufficient time, the Stockholm syndrome would kick in.

Chapter Twenty-Four

Alysia paced up and down the confining space as far as the chain would allow, ignoring the lingering wooziness. *Why didn't I rush him, stab him with the damn knife already?* Sure, it would be hard, make her go to a dark place she'd never wanted to go. But it had to be done. All that talk of his immortality had thrown her right off. Poe was certifiable. *No making sense of his way of thinking.* She just had to be better prepared next time. Get the jump on him. Literally.

She looked at the plate of eggs he'd brought. Were they drugged? Her stomach rumbled, squeezing into a painful knot from emptiness. It was unlikely he'd poisoned the food, because he could have gassed her just as easily. But then, nothing about that monster was easy. Talking about immortality like it was a given. If there was any justice, his very name would be struck from the annals of history as though he'd never lived. Never existed. If only that were true, so many more people would still be alive. Her parents, those two women. Who knew how many other victims there had been over the years?

Too sick to eat now, she slumped back onto the cot and curled up into a ball. She needed to rest while she could, be prepared to strike when the opportunity presented itself, and maybe even if it didn't. A last thought came to her before she drifted off — he'd looked different to her in some way. What was it? Yes. His two eyes matched in color now, both brown. Both hateful as ever.

She woke an indeterminable while later, disorientated. Realizing where she was, she pulled her legs up under her and rocked her body back and forth, something she hadn't done since she'd lost her parents. The lighting in the room had dimmed, only one bulb on now instead of the full string. But as she sat there, moving to the soothing rhythm, the full number of lights came on. She froze. Was he watching her? How could she not have realized that? Of course, he had a camera or cameras in the room. She looked up. Where? Damn, things were so small these days they could be hidden most anywhere. But it did warn her to be careful about the knife. The last thing she wanted was to alert the asshole to the fact that she had it on her person. The comfort it brought strapped to her leg? Priceless.

How much time had passed? There was no clock in the room, further disorientating her, reminded her of Vegas. *No. Don't go there. Don't bring any thoughts of a better time into this hellhole. Stay focused, Alysia. Think about escape. How to get the fuck out of here.*

* * * *

Nick had no idea what to do with the anger that fueled him other than to try to keep a tight lid on it. He and Walter had arrived back at his parents' house without any new leads to follow in finding out where Poe had holed up. Where he had taken Alysia. Just thinking of the man putting his hands on her made him want to drill the asshole right between the eyes. To think that she had saved his life when she could have ended it and he'd repaid her efforts by doing this to her? A murderous rage filled Nick, threatening his very sanity.

Walter even seemed to understand how extremely close to the edge of losing it he was, eyeing him with cautious glances whenever he made a sudden move. If that monster harmed a hair on her head, he was going down. He paced back and forth on the living room rug. No court of justice in the land was going to stop him from ending this thing. He should have done more, found the guy, taken him out already, illegal or not.

His stomach soured at his thoughts, which were unlike any he'd ever experienced before in his life. Sure, he always went after the bad guys for others that needed help. But this time, it was different. It was personal and the bad guy was threatening a woman he had fallen in love with. That was the wonder of it all — the love part. That he knew this was the woman he wanted to spend the rest of his life with, if she would have him. Three days had worked their magic for his grandparents. And now he completely understood how that could happen. He himself was living proof of the claim.

"Okay," he said making a decision and stopping his pacing. He turned to face his grandfather, who watched him from an armchair, sucking back on a whiskey bottle. "I can't hang around here. I'm going for a drive over to BC-STAR. Talk to her co-workers. Maybe someone knows something and doesn't realize it. If you need anything or hear anything, call me."

Walter's eyes were slightly glazed from the drink. "You find her, you bring her home, Nick. You hear me? If anyone can, you can. We're all counting on you."

He made an instant decision. As soon as this was over, he was getting help for the old man. He was drinking too much, that was obvious. Hell, they all were. This problem had only begun with the passing of his grandmother, Walter's beloved wife. He wanted more for his grandfather than a drunken slide into oblivion. He wanted to feel a closeness to him again, a sense of family, bring him into the fold. And he was certain he knew the woman who could help him.

But first he had to get Alysia back, rescue her from a madman. Feeling oddly like a hero in a classic novel from times of knights and dragons, he strode from the house to get on his steed, his modern-day horse, the black SUV. *Well, Christ, let me find that god-damn fire-breathing dragon so I can strike it down.*

He drove quickly toward BC-STAR, praying for his cell phone to ring with the exact location. He'd always been good at profiling who the UNSUB was, the unknown subject in an investigation. But this time, instead of having to answer the questions why and how to find out the who, he knew the full background of the bad guy. He looked up at the Costal Mountains he was driving through, desperate and hungry for answers. *Where are you hiding, Poe? You fucking coward.*

He parked at BC-STAR and got out into the deep chill of early morning. Six hours and twenty-two minutes had passed since she had gone missing. *Hang on, sweetheart, I'm coming.* His exhalations made frosty puffs of moist air about his face. *Wherever she is, I hope she's warm.* He looked up once more at the mountain range looming over the town of Hope. Below was the mighty Frazer River. It was picturesque in the right frame of mind. Not today. Not to him. Today it looked more like a black maze.

He strode into the front door of the office and right up to the front desk.

"May I help you, sir?" A woman looked over from her computer monitor and gave him a quick assessment. She appeared to like what she saw, endowing him with a wide smile of greeting.

"I'm Nick Wheeler, a friend of Alysia Rossini, and I need to ask you a few questions."

"How is Alysia? I heard about her house. Terrible thing." The young woman shook her head, a frown wiping away her smile. "Is she with you?"

"No, she's in trouble. I need answers from you and I need them quick."

"Sure. Okay. What do you need to know?" The woman's expression was serious, her blue eyes focused on him, her hands still on the countertop.

"When Alysia was here yesterday, someone gave her an envelope with black lettering on it—no return address. Does anyone know who dropped it off? It's crucial that I talk with them."

"Ah, yeah, that would be me. A guy dropped it off early yesterday morning."

"What guy? Would you recognize him again?"

"Probably. I got a good memory for faces. Names, not so much."

Nick pulled out his phone. He'd already downloaded a photo of the perp who'd bribed the pizza delivery guy.

Another woman came into the room carrying a heavy black bag. She gave them both a curious glance, setting the bag down on a chair.

He thumbed through his photos and held the phone out to the receptionist. "Was he the one?"

"Yeah. That's him. Big fellow. I don't live around here so I don't know many of the locals." She turned toward the other woman. "Emily, do you know this guy?" She showed the woman the photo.

"Uh, yeah, that's Arron Johnson. He works over at the hardware store. Moonlights at the Crossroads Bar as a bouncer."

Nick's heart leapt. *Great.* His first big break in the case.

"Thank you," he said, grabbing his phone back from the startled woman.

"What's going on? What kind of trouble is she in?"

"Alysia's in trouble?" Emily asked, her eyebrows knitting together.

"I don't have time to explain now, but I'll be back soon with answers. I promise." He raced to the door. No time to waste.

He jumped into his SUV and started the motor. If this Johnson fellow wasn't prepared to talk, he'd better be prepared for the beating of his life. Assault was a minor concern now that all bets were off.

He made Big Jim's, the only hardware store in town, in a couple of minutes, slamming on the brakes and parking in front. Half-running, he raced through the electronic doorway, looking all around for the asshole that had helped Poe. He spied a man stocking shelves in an aisle and hurried over to check him out and ask questions. The guy caught sight of him and turned to greet him. Nick saw the split second the guy recognized him. His prey turned and fled, running full tilt down the aisle, the cans of fruit he'd been stocking clattering to the ground and rolling onto the floor.

Nick took off after him. A couple of customers froze, watching the pantomime play out. In seconds they were at the back of the store. The store employee pushed through the swinging doors into the storage area, Nick right behind him.

"Stop!" he shouted. "I just want to ask you a few questions. A woman's life is at stake, for Christ's sake!"

The guy ignored him and kept running. He jerked to the right, stumbling around a pallet of goods stacked in the middle of the floor. It slowed him down just enough. Nick tackled him from behind. The cement was hard, and the man let out a yelp as he hit it. Nick grabbed his arms, pinning them to the floor. Another employee watched but didn't interfere.

"Now, tell me where Poe lives or, so help me God, I will break both your arms," he growled, his voice low and threatening. His body shook with adrenaline and he broke out in a light sweat.

"I don't have to tell you anything." The man spat the words out, though his face paled, his mouth pinched in a thin line from pain or worry. Didn't matter. He'd talk. Nick would make damn sure of that. With him involved with Poe, and Alysia gone, he had nothing to lose and everything to gain to find out where Poe had slithered back to. No matter what it took.

"You do. And you will." Nick pressed down harder on the man's arm.

"Stop that! You can't come in here and do that," the second employee said, finally waking up and walking over. He stood carefully out of the way, though. Good. He just needed a little time.

"This guy is involved with a man who kidnapped a woman early this morning. You don't get to tell me what I can and can't do."

The man looked undecided, hovering nearby. "Maybe you should cooperate, Arron. I mean, if a woman's missing…"

"And did you know that Poe killed her entire family? And of late killed two other women?"

"What? I don't believe you. Poe wouldn't do that. He's a survivalist, a guy who knows so much. He's taught me all manner of things." The man shook his head. "No way. You're making this up. How do I know you're not the bad guy? You come in here, attack *me*, for Christ's sake!"

Nick wanted to throttle him, but then he wouldn't be able to talk.

"Besides, I have no idea where Poe lives."

He was lying. Nick was one hundred percent positive. The guy closed his eyes when he said it, then looked down and away. Classic signs. And his gut agreed.

"I'm going to beat it out of you, so you'd better talk, buddy."

"Is it true that Poe killed some people?" the employee asked, coming closer.

"Yeah. I have proof. Do you know where I can find him?"

"Sorry. No idea."

Nick's patience was wearing thin. "I'm warning you. I'll break every damn bone in your body if I have to."

"Just try. You don't have proof. You're just farting in the wind."

"If I show you the proof, will you tell me Poe's location?"

For the first time Arron looked undecided. "Phhht. What ya got? Some made-up evidence? Crime scene photos? That's not proof."

Nick had had it. He pressed down harder on the man's arm.

"Owww," the man groaned. Nick felt a twinge of sympathy. He pushed it aside. This was the asshole defending a monster. Not worthy of sympathy.

"So help me God, I have no time for this! The clock is ticking. The monster has her right now. Tell me. *Now.* Last warning." Nick held on tighter, crouched on the man's stomach. Twisted his arm painfully. The guy moaned, then slumped back against the floor, defeated.

"Okay. Okay. He's up on Holy Cross Mountain. Bought a few acres under the name EAP Enterprises. It stands for Edgar Allan Poe. Jeffrey's got a thing for the writer. Damn near worships him. There's an old logging road you can take up there. But expect roadblocks. And it's under constant surveillance. I helped him install cameras. The guy's paranoid."

Nick immediately let him go. He stood.

He held out a hand to haul Arron to his feet. The guy ignored it. He rolled over and got up on his own, obviously trying to preserve what dignity he had left. He made a production of dusting his clothes off.

"You just might have saved a woman's life today," Nick said. He made his departure, striding back through the store and ignoring the stares of customers.

The name on the deed explained why Nils couldn't find the land title. He hadn't used his own name, but

the name of a phony business, most likely. *Clever move.*
Alysia had warned him the man liked to be a step
ahead of everyone. Not this time. *You're going down,
Poe.*

On the way to his vehicle he called up TETRAD.
"Nils, we got the location. The deed is in the name EAP
Enterprises. Up on Holy Cross Mountain. Text me the
coordinates. I'm on my way."

* * * *

Poe wasn't pleased with his subject. She hadn't eaten
the meal he'd gone to all the trouble of preparing. Just
sat there listless and rocking back and forth on the cot.
Perhaps she wasn't the one after all? He wanted a
woman of substance to carry on his bloodline. Was it
time to reconsider heading back to his original plan,
using her as another cog in his immortality?

Okay. He'd give her one day to prove her mettle, or
off to the hospital she'd go, become an unwilling organ
donor at best. Not that she'd know anything about it.
She'd be dead and gone. He narrowed his eyes, rubbing
at the one with the annoying contact. Such a shame
really, she was such a beautiful creature. Nature had
blessed her.

He pressed the heel of his palm into his throbbing
head. *Damn thing aching again.* She'd been so nice to him
as a child, too. Always smiling and making him feel
accepted. Something else he should be remembering.
But what? More and more, his brain was confining him.
He missed the man he'd been before the accident, when
his mind could always be relied on to expand at will.
Now, thinking was hard work. Gave him a fucking

headache. He slapped at his skull, willing the pain to stop.

He took a deep, cleansing breath. Keep control. Yes. Better. Force the pain down. Now. *Time to have a little chat with the guest of honor.*

He opened the door to her room. She got right up off the cot, looking warily at him, her expressions stronger.

"What do you want?" she demanded.

Good. She was back to herself.

"I want to have a little chat. Sit."

She crossed her arms over her chest. "I'll stand." The chain rattled as she moved a step closer. They both glanced down at it. "Such a big man to chain up a woman, eh?"

Anger filled him. *Damn insubordinate.* He rubbed at his head.

"Got a headache? That brain injury giving you grief? Too bad, so sad."

"You think you can anger me? Make me make a mistake? Not going to happen, sweetheart."

"Don't call me that," she spat.

"Why not?"

She didn't answer but glared at him.

"I'm here to offer you a choice. Take it. It's more than I gave the others. You should consider yourself lucky."

"Lucky?" she shouted. "Lucky to be chained up in a cellar with a madman?"

He took a step closer. "I'm not insane. I'm smarter than everyone else. You just don't get it. You don't understand how the universe works."

"Enlighten me then."

"Are you on birth control?" He checked out her body deliberately, glancing up and down at her figure. She shrank into herself a bit. He enjoyed the power.

"Why do you ask that?"

"Just need to know if I can offer you the choice."

"What choice?"

"You first. Are you on anything?" He watched her wrestle within herself.

"No. I use condoms when I hook up." She didn't look at him when she said it, her face flushing a dull red.

"Nothing to be ashamed of. But that means I can offer you a choice. My child or becoming an organ donor."

"What? What on earth does that even mean?"

"You don't know? I dropped off the two women at hospitals in Vancouver to be used as parts for needy patients. Fresh organ donors. Quite the plan, don't you think? Never been done before in the annals of history. I'm sure the authorities have no idea what to make of that. What to make of me. But I'd bet my bottom dollar they didn't waste the opportunity to harvest the useful bits." He smiled his satisfaction as her expression turned to one of out-and-out horror.

"How could you do such a thing? It's monstrous! Fucking evil!" she screamed in his face. His head began hurting, far more. The blood pounded inside his brain. How could it hurt so much? He closed his eyes, but that only made the room spin.

He swayed, unsteady on his feet. He lurched a step or two forward, unable to get his bearings. She grabbed at him. His vision narrowed, faltered, but he caught the glimmer of steel. Why was there a knife in her hand? Where had it come from?

A sudden movement and his legs went out from under him. He fell to the floor on his knees. She stood over him, the knife clenched in her fist.

A sensation of wetness on his leg. He fumbled to touch his thigh. His hand came away covered in blood.

Nausea roiled his stomach, made him want to puke. He held it in with difficulty. He turned his anger on her.

"You stabbed me, you fucking bitch!"

Chapter Twenty-Five

"I'll do it again if you don't let me out of here," Alysia threatened Poe, standing over him. She could hardly believe she had done it, but it hadn't been as hard to do as she'd thought once he'd threatened her...and told her what he had done to the others. *Vile.*

"No getting out of here, bitch. You're buried — deep underground. No one will ever find you."

She widened her eyes at the new information and hesitated. She still had need of him. She had to get out of here. Everything good in her life awaited topside.

"Might as well give up. It's all over for you. Maybe you'll get to see your family again. Or not. Who knows what's next?"

"You're going straight to hell!" She had never hated him more for what he was making her do.

"Tsk-tsk. You think you're the only one who's tried to send me there?" He looked at his leg. The bloodstain was spreading. "I think you might have nicked an artery. Maybe we'd better apply a stopgap measure.

You let me bleed out and you'll never get out of here alive."

She swallowed, hesitating. Then she went to her bunk and picked up the sheet. She tried tearing it to make a bandage, but the fabric wouldn't give. "Damn it," she cursed. She tore at it with the knife, making a bloody mess, but managed to tear off a narrow strip.

"Better hurry. Unless you want me to die? Makes you the same as me then, bitch."

"I'm nothing like you! I won't *ever* become an unfeeling monster who kills people." "Don't move." She worked the cloth around his upper thigh, tying the ends together tightly, manufacturing a makeshift tourniquet. She sat back on her haunches. "There. Now what? We have to get you to the hospital or you'll bleed out. You don't look so good."

"I don't think that's going to happen. Might as well sit back and enjoy the show. I'm a goner anyway. Got a bullet in my brain. Aneurism. Doctors said it was just a matter of time until my best-before date expires. Might as well make this my Alamo. Yours too."

Her breath froze in her chest. He was deadly serious, but oscillating from one idea to the other so quickly that he made her head spin. He was right about one thing. He was going to die if help didn't arrive soon. He planned to take her with him. *Fuck no.* She wouldn't accept that. She shook her head violently. "No way. You're not taking me down with you. Where's the key? You got it on you?"

She leaned over him and began rummaging in his pockets. He had a scanner clipped to his belt that was no good, and she threw it on the cot. She found nothing of use to her like a well-charged cell phone. He weakly tried to stop her, but she fended him off, slapping at his hands. "I won't let you die. I'll never let you change who I am. What I stand for."

She realized at that moment, faced with the choice again of letting him die or helping him live, she would do the same, *was* doing the same. She was here on earth to save people, not harm them. Not that she regretted stabbing him in self-defense. But that was as far as it went. Now she had to see him put to rights with medical help. The law could take care of him after that. His guilt was obvious.

"Someone may take your life away. But it won't be me. You'll be killing yourself if you don't help me get you out of here."

The knowledge gave her an unexpected sense of peace even as she faced the new worry of how to get out of the bunker—alive. She had to get back to Nick. Every fiber of her being wanted that. Craved it. Demanded it. He was the man for her. No doubt remained in her mind. He was the one who applauded her, who tried to protect her. Would have achieved it if it had been humanly possible. Not his fault they were dealing with such a clever SOB. A monster. A freak of nature. A psychopath without morals or ethics.

"Not go…ing to…help you. Stay…put." His words sounded slurred now. He was in a bad way. Nothing in his pockets. She gave him a slight shake. "Tell me how to get you out of here. Where's the key? Come on! You need to tell the media about what you've done. We may never be found otherwise. Then no one will ever know about the deal you struck with the devil to gain your immortality. Go down in the history books as the most brilliant mind of them all." She hated his perverted logic, but it might motivate him to allow her to help him. *Talk about twisted.*

"Hmm...no...not go...ing to work. My memoirs.... Left notes...a friend will see me pub...lished. Nice...try. You die." He lapsed into unconsciousness. *Oh, God, now what?*

* * * *

Nick found the old, abandoned logging road, hidden as it was by trees and bushes. They had regrown since the lumber company that had the lease for the old-growth forest had moved on. He stopped the SUV, got out and undid the chains that had been placed across the road between two large stakes, ignoring the *Keep Out, Private Property* sign. He jumped back into his vehicle and tore up the mountainside, the SUV's tires spinning out a few times from the steepness of the incline, bouncing over rocks and debris.

Who wants to live in such a difficult-to-reach part of the world? Only someone wanting to hide from it and do his disgusting deeds in private. He shook his head in dismay, his muscles tightening under the stress. He waited impatiently for Nils to call again. The entire TETRAD team were on their way. Law enforcement would only be informed when they knew what they were dealing with. They had a better chance of saving her without the local law detachment getting in the way and further upsetting Poe. Safer for everyone.

He just had to keep moving. If only he could send her some kind of mind message, let her know help was on the way. *Hang on, Alysia, I'm going to find you if I have to tear the top off this bloody mountain.*

The phone rang and he reached for it. His nerves were so jumpy he almost dropped the device back onto the dash.

"Yeah."

"Nick. Okay. Records indicate EAP Enterprises bought two shipping containers. He also leased a large bulldozer from BC Powell Equipment, though it must have been some nightmare getting heavy equipment up the mountainside. What's the road like?"

"Steep, but not impassable. Built wider as well for the logging trucks that would have used it."

"We're halfway to Hope. Should be there within forty minutes."

"I'm just about there. Call me when you arrive."

"Be careful, buddy."

Nick hung up. So far, he'd only seen evidence of cameras at the chained entrance. It would be a large area to keep track of all comings and goings. *Hopefully too large.* A few hundred more meters and the trees opened to reveal the yard site. A large packed-dirt area about fifty meters square, it surrounded a large white yurt with a deck perched on the edge of the mountain. An outbuilding stood to one side, along with an array of solar panels. He parked on the roadside just before the treeline, drew his Glock from its underarm holster, checked the safety was off and jumped out. He worked his way around the stand of trees and bushes toward the yurt. There was ample evidence of cameras mounted on the sides of trees.

There would be no element of surprise. Not if Poe was watching for intruders. Or maybe he was too busy? The thought made him want to puke. That asshole was going down this time. Never again would he be allowed to hurt a woman. Even if it meant he himself was charged for it. To get the monster who had killed Alysia's parents and two other women, it would be

worth it to spend time in prison. Best-case scenario —
manslaughter in self-defense. He'd only do a few years.

He worked his way around to the back of the yurt,
but all he heard were the sounds of the snow crunching
under his boots and the call of the ravens as they
scavenged for food. A rare black fox crossed his path at
the edge of the evergreen trees, scurrying away as soon
as he was spotted. Chills raced up and down his spine.
Any second he expected gunshots — with his name on
them. But nothing happened. He made it right up to the
door of the structure. He slipped inside, gun cocked,
safety off.

"*Grrrr.*" Growling, back-of-the-neck-hair-raising,
throaty sounds came from a large wolfdog lying on a
chunk of rug. The large animal scrambled to all fours
and faced Nick, its sharp canine teeth bared by its
pulled-back lips.

Please don't make me shoot you.

In the couple of seconds he had at most before the dog
leapt, he gave a quick look around. The yurt was wide
open inside, without any partitions between rooms. No
one was inside. He slammed the door shut just as the
dog made for him, managing it with a split second to
spare. He let out a low sigh. *Whew, too close.*

He spied the outbuilding and crossed the short
distance over to it. He kicked open the door, gun at the
ready. The building was empty except for shelves of
tools, oil cans and equipment. *Where the hell did he take
her?* Frustrated, he knocked some of the tins off a shelf.
They clattered to the floor.

Okay. He stood outside the door and looked around.
The two shipping containers. He needed to figure out
where they were. In a stroke of inspiration, it hit him
that maybe they were buried. He'd gotten a bulldozer

up here. There should be some indication on the ground, right? But though he walked the entire area, there were no obvious signs of a dig. As he finished the perusal of the landscape, a large vehicle was pulling into the yard.

He strode over and watched Jake and Quinn disembark from one side of the sturdy Hummer, Cole and Nils from the other, all wearing tactical gear. He let out a sigh of relief that they were there, on his side. Cole carried an extra bulletproof vest in one hand. The best help a man could ask for had just arrived.

"I've secured the area. No signs of activity." Nick filled his team in without wasting any time on the pleasantries. He took the black Kevlar vest from Cole, slipped off his winter jacket and pulled it on, then tugged his winter coat over the top, leaving the zipper open. "No obvious entrance to any containers. I'm thinking they were buried. He's covered his tracks well."

Jake took out his phone. "I'll order ground-penetrating radar equipment to be sent up." He turned away and began speaking into his phone.

Cole and Quinn strode off to get the lie of the land. Nils came closer, his nose reddened by the cold, a knit cap pulled over his head and ears. Nick hardly noticed the biting wind, which was rougher at this high elevation. It was all he could do to keep himself together. "If he uses anything technical, I'll be able to pinpoint his exact location," Nils said.

"I don't see him being that stupid. But you never know." Nick shrugged, giving him his honest assessment.

"Yeah, I know what you mean. But you did say he had brain damage. It's always possible that he'll fuck up."

"True. But I'm not counting on it. God, Nils, I'm going crazy here." He rubbed at his neck. It had grown stiff from the overwhelming stress. "What if—"

"Don't go there, buddy," Nils interrupted. "No point. Alysia's a trauma nurse, right? She's tough. She'll hold her own just fine. He's been after her for years and she's still standing. Keep the faith. We're going to find her alive. Focus on that."

"Working on it."

Alysia checked for Jeffrey's vital signs, pushing herself to lay two fingers against his neck. She was repulsed by physically touching him, but worked to ignore it. His heartbeat was faint, but there. She hated being in this situation. She yanked at the chains that kept her from helping to save his life. They rattled against the metal. If she couldn't get free or if Nick didn't find them soon, Poe would die. She ignored the little voice inside that said, *Why give a fuck about that outcome? The bastard deserves all that and more.* Maybe. But it wasn't her call. Not anymore. She'd beat him at his own game and he would not turn her into a monster. Not now, not ever. She had too much to live for. She had looked into the abyss and she was set free by her own will. Her choice.

And Kate needed her. Nick would be fine once he'd calmed down, she reassured herself. She could talk him into giving her another chance. Hell, even Walter could use some help. Give him some nice Sunday dinners to make up for his recent losses. *Dinner with a family can do a heart a lot of good.* It triggered the memory of how she'd treasured those times with her parents.

Tears welled in her eyes. What she wouldn't give for one more Sunday dinner. She shook them away angrily. She would start up the tradition again. Quit hiding behind her life with working and drinking and acting out of control. If she lived through this, she was making big changes. *If?* A terrible fear chilled her body. Surely they would find her? *But what if they can't locate Poe's land? Then what?*

She looked at the rusty metal ceiling. Was anyone coming for her? She swallowed the lump of fear tightening her throat. *Please, God, if you can hear me, it's Alysia. I need your help. Please, let Nick find me. Guide him to me. I'll turn over a new leaf. Work at becoming a better person. Please, I don't want to die here with a madman.*

She couldn't ask for leniency for Poe. That was beyond her. Leave it to a higher power. Maybe one day she'd forgive him, but she wouldn't count on it. It was enough that she hadn't killed him. That he hadn't turned her into something she wasn't. A killer.

She'd stayed true to herself — the most she could ask for. But not dying, that was right up there at the top of her list of wishes. Well at the very least, her capture had saved someone else. He'd never get to kidnap and kill anyone else. Not now. Not ever.

She looked over at Poe. His breathing had worsened. Harsh gasps that made her clench her teeth together. She had no medicine, nothing that she could do. It went against everything she stood for. She was the one who always ran in first to a scene, started the meds as soon as possible. To be so hamstrung hurt her to the core. Would they have to endure hours, days of this torture? No, Poe wouldn't last days.

Her mind froze up with the idea. Numb, she sat and let the horror wash over her. She trembled, unable to stop her limbs from shaking with fear. A faint noise drew her attention. Something had fallen over. Above her head. She was certain of it. She looked around frantically. What could she bang on the wall with? Nothing of real substance that would make a loud sound. All she had on the cot was her useless cell phone and a scanner.

She stared at them as if they could answer the fundamental question of the universe that every person asked at least once in their lifetime — why am I here? *To survive this — that's for damn certain if nothing else.* Then, suddenly, an idea was rising to the surface of her mind. What Nick had shared with her about graphene. About it being the new wonder material. That all cars would be equipped with it in the future, their bodies becoming batteries that could be charged in a couple of minutes instead of hours. The very thing that was holding back electric cars from expanding all over the planet. What if the scanner had a nine-volt battery? Her mind quickened.

Then her hands began working with frantic motions as her brain saw the solution in one flash of pure, utter brilliance, driven by desperation. She opened the back of the small black box that was the scanner, breaking a nail off in the process of prying up the plastic housing, but the reveal of a nine-volt battery took all the sting out of it. Duracell. *Oh my, Mr. Bunny, you're on.*

She tugged the metal bobby pins from her hair, scraping off the plastic ends and straightening the bent metal into one long piece, abusing another fingernail in the process. Alysia grabbed the small battery and held the lengthened pins to its positive and negative polls.

They'd do. She warmed the phone case with hand friction to get the electrons moving, remembering that part from a high-school science class.

Okay. The moment of truth.

The Nobel guys had said they'd gotten five minutes of charge in that first experiment with a single row of graphite-creating graphene on sticky tape. She just needed twenty seconds. Taking a deep breath, she held the metal pins connecting to the battery to her phone case, creating a full circuit.

Please. Please. Please. Sweat was dripping and stinging her eyes, her heart thudding so loud a freight train of white noise was bouncing around in her head.

The screen lit up. Her fingers trembling almost uncontrollably, she touched the screen a few times until the device was ringing Nick's number.

"Alysia! Is that you?" His voice just about did her in. But there was no time to waste.

"Nick! I heard you. There was some noise above my head. I'm underground. In a shipping container. Need an ambulance." She had to shout the words, unable to hold the phone to her face. It was a delicate process keeping all the random parts together as it was. She heard Poe moaning and she glanced over at him. There was so little time left. How long would it take to find the entrance or dig her out?

"Alysia! Thank God. Where underground? Under what?"

"I don't know. But I heard something. Did you knock something over? Oh my, it's so good to hear your voice."

The phone died, the screen going black. *NO.* She swallowed hard, placing a hand to her throat. Had he understood? Did Nick know where to look?

"Nick, I just got a signal! That phone I gave you, the one with the graphene case. It's coming from underground. Close by," Nils shouted.

Nick turned to Nils, who was running toward him, his expression lit up with hope and intensity.

"Alysia just called. Not sure why it took so long. Maybe the battery was low? I hadn't charged it in a couple of days," he said.

"Or, if the battery has died, she might have figured out how to rig the phone. That's my bet. You said she was one smart cookie."

"Okay. She said she heard a noise. Not sure when — Yes! I was in the machine shed and threw some stuff around." Nick began running toward the main door of the building. Inside, he looked around frantically. The entrance had to be here somewhere. But where? His brothers-in-arms joined him to scramble around the space, throwing things out of the way.

"Shit! She said she needed an ambulance." How had he forgotten that? Was she hurt? She'd sounded strong. But that was just Alysia being true to who she was.

Jake stopped working and pulled out his phone. "I'll call," he said, then spoke into his phone. He hung up. "BC-STAR's on the way. They can land in the yard — told them it's large enough for a helicopter. No overhead wires. Living off-grid has its advantages."

"Fuck! Where's the damn entrance?" Nick was ready to tear out his hair. He rummaged around between the benches, looking for the key. He scratched and bruised his hands in his haste, hardly noticing the pain of driving slivers into the palm of his hand. It was nothing compared to what Alysia was going through. *Please, God, let her be okay.*

He scrabbled frantically along under a bench's edge. He kept pressing and heard a click of something engaging. Suddenly the unit began moving, a grinding sound of a motor accompanying the maneuver. An opening appeared in the shed's floor. A ladder was attached to one side, allowing access to the bottom.

"Here! I've found it!" he shouted and began his quick scramble to the bottom, nearly wiping out on the metal railings in his haste. Ignoring the last few rungs, he jumped down onto the floor of the container, his boots making a ringing sound when they hit the corrugated metal.

He took a second to pull his gun again, ready for whatever lay ahead. No one was in the first unit, but he spotted a doorway to another space. *They must be in there.* His gun braced in both hands, he peered inside. Alysia stood a few feet away from the doorway, waiting, her expression tight and haunted.

He looked around the space. He would not lower his guard until he was absolutely certain Poe was incapacitated, much as he wanted to drop everything, grab hold of her and never let her go. He noted the killer was on the floor near her feet, not moving. Blood pooled around him. He appeared unconscious. Sweat dripped into his eyes, which he blinked out of the way. Nothing would make him more satisfied than emptying a full clip into the guy, but the man was down for the count, so there was no point in it.

"Is he alive?" he asked, moving forward to check, keeping his gun pointed at Poe.

"Yes, barely. He's unarmed. Don't shoot."

It was safe. He could take a few seconds. He moved forward as though he was in a dream to take Alysia into his arms. The feeling was indescribable, holding her close to his heart.

"Thank the heavens you're okay," he murmured into her hair, breathing in her intoxicating essence. Even now, he kept one eye on Poe. When the others streamed into the room, he finally relaxed and enjoyed the precious moments that were beyond compare, turning his full attention to Alysia. Within a few minutes he had located the key and unlocked the chain, setting her free.

"I don't want him to die. I could have ended him — but I didn't." She looked up at him as she said it, almost as though she was trying to understand.

"I told you, you're a straight shooter, though I don't think anyone would have blamed you if you had. I'm proud of you, beautiful. Figuring out how to make the cell phone work." He'd noted her handiwork on the cot. His chest did indeed fill with a rush of pride as he stood holding this remarkable woman in his arms. Not only beautiful, but clever, too. His favorite type, with maybe more emphasis on intelligent, something he most admired.

They ignored the TETRAD team unceremoniously picking up Poe, then exiting with him. Nick and Alysia trailed behind them, their arms wrapped tightly around each other's waists. He'd taken off his coat and helped her into it to keep her warm.

They stood holding each other as the BC-STAR helicopter arrived, waving off any and all offers of help.

"I'm perfectly fine," she declared, giving the crew a thumbs-up.

"That you are, my beautiful, *beautiful* woman. I love you," he said, giving her a smile that left no doubt as to what he was feeling.

She laid a gentle hand on his face, stared intently into his eyes. "Did you just say you love me after knowing each other for three days?"

"Yup. Good enough for my grandparents — good enough for me. If you'll have me?"

"Hmm. You promise to make it last fifty-plus years? And to take me to Scotland?"

"I do. Do you promise to make it last fifty-plus years? And let me install a sex swing?"

"I do. And, furthermore, I promise to cook Sunday dinners for our family for all the years of our lives. I love you too, Nick. Now and for always."

"Oh, my beautiful Alysia." He kissed her then, capturing those soft, sweet lips with his own. He experienced a sensation of euphoria right down to the tips of his toes. *Life. It doesn't get any better.*

Chapter Twenty-Six

Three months later

"Edinburgh Castle. Not too shabby, Mr. Wheeler," Alysia said. They stood, holding hands and looking out over a battlement and toward the old town of Edinburgh. She admired the panoramic view from their vantage point on top of Castle Rock, a fortress built on a volcanic structure that had stood for nearly a millennium. Centuries and centuries of occupancy beneath her feet took her breath away. But nothing was as exciting and overwhelming as the man who had arranged the tour and who stood by her side, her equal partner and protector. What better place to have that promised dance?

He kissed the back of her hand, his lips eliciting a shiver of excitement that danced along her skin. She'd never get enough of this man. "Thank you, Mrs. Wheeler. Nothing too good for my new wife. Just hoping she comes to work for us at TETRAD so I can have access to her every moment of every day."

"I've been thinking about that."

"And?" he prompted, giving her the full benefit of his arresting eyes that made her want to do anything he asked. *So unfair.*

She took a deep breath. "Yes. I say yes."

He crushed her to him. "Thank you. You won't be sorry. You'll be such a valuable addition to our team. I know it means giving up something you love. You sure you're okay with that?"

"Definitely. I'll still be helping others. Just in a different capacity. It's time." The job had been taking such a toll. She wanted to pull back from the extreme stress of finding others in the worst shape of their lives. *Fairly common, really.* Trauma nurses in the field had a short lifespan.

Nick took her into his arms. He used a hand to brush back a strand of hair that had blown loose from her ponytail. The air swirling about the thick castle walls had turned into a stiff breeze. It made her think of ghosts, but thankfully they were all gone now. Her nemesis was in jail, unlikely to get out in her lifetime. And even less likely to live much longer with his acute health concerns. But the greatest miracle of all? Her friend Kate had rallied, gone into remission and was holding her own. For now. It was a gift from God. She'd never ask for another.

She stood on tiptoe in response to his gentle caress, holding her face up for the expected kiss. Instead, he traced his fingers lightly over her cheeks, her nose and her chin before running one finger across her lips. "You are so beautiful, so kind and giving. How did I get so lucky?" His voice was low and husky, filled with the raw power of being completely in love. Between them, they had driven the bogeyman away and begun a new life filled with strong promise for a good future.

"I don't know. Uh, maybe because you deserve me? You're the best person in the world for me. Kind, intelligent, handsome and wise. With a funny grandfather to boot, to keep it all interesting. My very own golden man. You make my heart smile."

Walter was never boring, that was certain. But he'd come around too. Especially since she'd instituted mandatory Sunday dinners. Often, other members of TETRAD joined them. And Kate, of course. They were all becoming one big family. It was awesome. More than she had allowed herself to hope for.

"Stop, you'll give me a big head," he teased, a wide grin on his handsome mug.

"No, I'll never stop. I'll love you the same all our lives. Maybe more. No, make that definitely more every day we share together."

His eyes reddened and tears welled up in her own. "I love you, Alysia. More than you can ever know."

"And I love you, Nick, more than you can ever know."

Want to see more from this author?
Here's a taster for you to enjoy!

Manitoba Tea & Tarot Mysteries: Magic, Mayhem & Murder
January Bain

Excerpt

*The most beautiful thing we can experience is the mysterious.
It is the source of all true art and science. — Albert Einstein*

Thirteen years ago

"Will she let us stay?" Tulip's eyes widened, her nose
and cheeks reddened by the freezing wind. My triplet
shivered, wiping her dripping nose on the back of her
red mitten. I straightened the collar on her worn jacket
and tucked the thin scarf around her neck. The snow
was falling more heavily now, already filling in the
tracks the three of us had made walking from the street
light to the front stoop, the warning still ringing in my
head. *'Don't knock until you've counted to a hundred if you
know what's good for you.' Twelve, thirteen, fourteen...*

"I'm not sure, but if we're really, really good, she
might. At least for tonight," I interrupted my counting
to answer her.

"Yeah, don't you be backtalking her like you did to
Mommy," Star said, staring accusingly.

"I never did that!" Tulip's bottom lip started to quiver.

"Hush, no one is at fault," I said. If she started bawling, I didn't know how long I could hold off. My throat had a lump in it big as a baseball. *Thirty-one, thirty-two, thirty-three.*

Star screwed up her face but held her tongue, though only after I gave her my sternest older-sister look. I'd been born at one minute to midnight, making me the oldest sister by a full day. Not that birthdays were ever celebrated, though we'd had eight already. Mommy said we were too much trouble on a regular day. No way was she holding a two-day party for a trio of brats.

I tugged the paper sack holding all our possessions closer to my chest, thinking of the one precious book and the half-box of Pop-Tarts Mommy had tucked inside for our supper. Maybe Granny would have a toaster or a stove element to warm them up? Or maybe she might have some juice or pop? My throat was dry. Even water would taste good.

Star stamped her feet to stay warm, her pink running shoes leaving an intricate pattern from the soles as she packed the snow. Her scarf had icicles forming from her warm breath hitting the frosty air and her cheeks shone bright red. No frostbite — not yet anyway. But the wind was picking up, blowing showers of ice crystals off the roof and onto our bare heads.

Sixty-six, sixty-seven. I glanced across the open field between Granny's house and the house next door, visualizing wolves coming out of the evergreens of the thick forest and circling the town. We'd been dropped off on one of the coldest days of the year. Minus forty-seven, according to the loud man on the radio in our old van. I'd caught the name of the town on the welcoming sign leading in. *Snowy Lake, population 1259.*

I was proud to be the first one to learn to read, first one to do most things. Then I could help my little sisters, when they'd let me.

Eighty-nine, ninety. I was shaking now, could barely keep from kicking at the door with my foot. But a promise is a promise. If Mommy came back and saw me doing wrong, I'd get a swat for sure. *You know she's not coming back, right?* a small voice inside me piped up, making tears well. *No! Don't ever say that.* Hard as times had been, Mommy loved us deep down inside. *She's coming back. One day.* When things were better for her, she'd be back. She promised. And if I kept my solemn promise to look after my sisters, then everything would be okay. It had to be.

"Okay, let's not forget who we are. The awesome McCalls. Okay, time's up."

Just as I reached one hundred the back-porch light came on, a beacon in the darkness, spotlighting the three of us huddled in the dark.

"Land's sake alive, what are the three of you doing outside waiting in the snow?"

I spoke up, holding out the bedraggled piece of paper with the slightly smeared ink. "Granny Toogood, my mommy said to give you this."

If she was surprised at me calling her Granny, she didn't show it. She took the offering and read it with an intense expression. I peeked at her while she read. Dark curls gleamed around a soft face. She was wearing a nice pair of blue slacks with a matching blouse over a slim body, no stains or holes. *She must be rich.* She was shorter than Mommy, too. When she glanced down at Star, Tulip and me, the expression in her blue eyes was kind, as though she was very sure of something. I liked her immediately. I badly wanted her to like me, too. Then maybe she would feel obliged to help my sisters.

"Well, let's get you all inside then," she said, refolding and tucking the letter into her pants pocket.

I waited until my sisters had clamored in the doorway before I glanced back at the forest. The pack of wolves had vanished.

Home of Erotic Romance

Sign up for our newsletter and find out about all our romance book releases, eBook sales and promotions, sneak peeks and FREE romance books!

About the Author

January Bain has wished on every falling star, every blown-out birthday candle and every coin thrown in a fountain to be a storyteller. To share the tales of high adventure, mysteries, and full-blown thrillers she has dreamed of all her life. The story you now have in your hands is the compilation of a lot of things manifesting itself for this special series. Hundreds of hours spent researching the unusual and the mundane have come together to create a series that features strong women who don't take life too seriously, wild adventures full of twists and unforeseen turns, and hot complicated men who aren't afraid to take risks. She can only hope the stories of her beloved Brass Ringers will capture your imagination as much as they did hers when she wrote them.

If you are looking for January Bain, you can find her hard at work every morning without fail in her office with two furry babies trying to prove who does a better job of guarding the doorway. And, of course, she's married to the most romantic man! Who once famously replied to her inquiry about buying fresh flowers for their home every week, "Give me one good reason why not?" Leaving her speechless and knocking her head against the proverbial wall for being so darn foolish. She loves flowers.

January loves to hear from readers. You can find her contact information, website details and author profile page at https://www.totallybound.com